REFUGEE
TALES

Edited by
David Herd & Anna Pincus

First published in Great Britain in 2016 by Comma Press.
www.commapress.co.uk

'The Detainee's Tale' was first published in *The Guardian* (28 June, 2015).
'The Refugee's Tale' was first published in *Beached Here at Random by Mysterious Forces: 50 Years of Poetry at the University of Kent* (University of Kent, 2015), edited by Ben Hickman and Janet E Montefiore. A version of pages 135-138 of the 'Afterword' first appeared in the *Los Angeles Review of Books* (3 March, 2015).

The opinions of the authors and editors are not necessarily those of the publisher. A CIP catalogue record of this book is available from the British Library.

ISBN   1910974234
ISBN-13   978 1910974230

Proceeds from this book go to the following two charities:
Gatwick Detainees Welfare Group and Kent Refugee Help.

The publisher gratefully acknowledges assistance from Arts Council England.

Set in Bembo 11/13 by David Eckersall.

Contents

PROLOGUE   v

THE MIGRANT'S TALE   1
Dragan Todorovic

THE CHAPLAIN'S TALE   13
Michael Zand

THE UNACCOMPANIED MINOR'S TALE   17
Inua Ellams

THE LORRY DRIVER'S TALE   25
Chris Cleave

THE ARRIVER'S TALE   35
Abdulrazak Gurnah

THE VISITOR'S TALE   41
Hubert Moore

THE DETAINEE'S TALE   49
Ali Smith

CONTENTS

THE INTERPRETER'S TALE 63
Carol Watts

THE APPELLANT'S TALE 69
David Herd

THE DEPENDANT'S TALE 85
Marina Lewycka

THE FRIEND'S TALE 93
Jade Amoli-Jackson

THE DEPORTEE'S TALE 99
Avaes Mohammad

THE LAWYER'S TALE 107
Stephen Collis

THE REFUGEE'S TALE 125
Patience Agbabi

Afterword: Walking with Refugee Tales 133
About the Contributors 144

Prologue

This prologue is not a poem
It is an act of welcome
It announces
That people present
Reject the terms
Of a debate that criminalises
Human movement
It is a declaration
This night in Shepherdswell
Of solidarity.

It says that we have started –
That we are starting out –
That by the oldest action
Which is listening to tales
That other people tell
Of others
Told by others
We set out to make a language
That opens politics
Establishes belonging
Where a person dwells.
Where they are now
Which is to say
Where we are now
Walking
In solidarity

Along an ancient track
That we come back to the geography of it
North of Dover
That where
The language starts
Now longen folk to goon
On this pilgrimage.

In June not April
And with the sweet showers far behind us
Though with the birds singing
And people sleeping
With open eye
And what we long for
Is to hear each others' tales
And to tell them again
As told by some hath holpen
Walking
So priketh hem nature
Not believing the stories
Our officials tell.
Because we know too much
About what goes unsaid
And what we choose to walk for
Is the possibility of trust
In language
To hear the unsaid spoken
And then repeated
Made
Unambiguous and loud
Set out over a landscape gathered
Step by step
As by virtue of walking which
We call our commons
Every sap vessel bathed in moisture
And what that commons calls for
Is what these stories sound.

Of crossing
For to seken straunge strondes
In moments of emergency
Whan that they were seeke
Of tribunals
Where the unsaid goes unspoken
Lines of questioning
No official has written down
People present by video
Answers mistranslated
As outside by the station
At the dead of morning
As the young sun rises
Woken in their homes
People are picked up and detained.
Routinely and
Arbitrarily
In every holt and heeth
Under the sun while
Smale fowles maken melodye
And why we walk is
To make a spectacle of welcome
This political carnival
Across the Weald of Kent
People circulating
Making music
Listening to stories
People urgently need said.

And said
And said again
Stories of the new geography
Stories of arrival
Of unaccompanied minors
Of people picked up and detained
Of process

And mistranslation
Networks of visitors and friends
This new language we ask for
Forming
Strung out
Along the North Downs Way.

Which makes it a question of scale.
Consider just
The scale
Of the undertaking
Chaucer's pilgrims crossing
Palatye and Turkye and Ruce
Across the Grete See
Which is the Mediterranean
Dark these days
Not like wine
Crossing through Flaundres
Through Artoys
Crossing the water at Pycardie.
And all the while finding stories
And then all of them
Gathering one night in London
And so the Host says
Since we're walking
Why don't we tell each other tales
And so they do
Out of Southwark
And what comes out of Southwark
Is a whole new language
Of travel and assembly and curiosity
And welcome.

To make his English sweete.
That's why Chaucer told his tales.
How badly we need English
To be made sweet again

Rendered hostile by act of law
So that even friendship is barely possible –
Ther as this lord was kepere of the celle –
So we might actually talk
And in talking
Come to understand the journey –
Tender
Says the poet
To Canterbury they wende.

Tender
To hold
From the French
Tendre
From the English
For listening
To a story as it is said
To attend
Tendre
And then writing it down
Because it isn't written
Because the hearings
In the British immigration system
Are not courts
Of record.
So there are no stories
And people leave
As if there never had been
Stories
And so nobody
Who reaches a verdict
Has a real story
With which to contend
So now we are telling them
En masse
And people will listen

In sondry londes
And specially
From every shires ende.

But this prologue is not a poem
It is an act of introduction
Bathed every veyne in swich licour
And all the introduction can do
Is set the tone
Albeit the tone
Is everything
And the tone is welcoming
And the tone is celebratory
And the tone is courteous
And the tone is real
And every step sets out a demand
And every demand is urgent
And what we call for
Is an end
To this inhuman discourse.

And so we stop this night
And the Host steps up
And he says
Listen to this story
Whan that Aprill with his shoures soote
And the room goes quiet
And a voice starts up
And then the language
Alters
Sweet
Tender
Perced to the roote.

David Herd

The Migrant's Tale

as told to

Dragan Todorovic

HEERE BEGYNNETH THE MIGRANT his tale.

#

In Syria once upon a time dwelt a company of rich merchants, trustworthy and true.[1]

#

We are sitting on the second floor of a corner office in Birmingham. This is an area of white shirts and Pink Floyd streets. Metal blinds are all down. I put the chocolate cake I've brought for Aziz on the coffee table connecting the three of us, and it feels inappropriate. Cream over pain.

Our interpreter wears a dark suit and his stern beard makes him look worried. Aziz is dressed in loosely fitting clothes, at least a size bigger. He speaks English, I was told, but feels safer if the interpreter is with us.

I would like to start as far as possible from the recent events in his life, so I ask about his childhood in Syria. What were his favourite toys? The interpreter must have used the word 'game' when speaking of toys and Aziz says, 'I was a basketball player, a team captain. My family was big and important. We were wealthy, and never had any problems that I can remember.'

#

O sudden woe, you are ever successor to worldly bliss, sprinkled with bitterness, the end of the joy in the fruit of our labour! Woe waits at the end of our gladness. Hear this counsel for your own safety: on happy days do remember the misery that waits behind.

#

He grew up in Daraa, in the south of Syria, the city first mentioned in the Egyptian documents some 35 centuries ago. Moses fought his battles here, but that was yesterday. Today, Daraa is the place where the Syrian uprising started when 15 schoolchildren were arrested for doing graffiti, in March 2011.

That is an area frequented by despots, droughts, and deities. A hundred kilometres to the north and south lie two capitals: Damascus and Amman. Jerusalem is close; Judaism and Christianity and Islam walk on the same streets, shop in the same souks. Fall silent in the afternoon heat, scream at one another when they wake up.

#

Now it happened that these rich merchants decided to visit Rome – whether for business or for pleasure they would not say. They stayed in that town a certain time, fulfilling their desires. And it so happened that they heard of the excellent renown of the emperor's daughter, Lady Custance[2]. [...] The common report was that she was beautiful without pride, young without folly, humble and courteous – the most beautiful woman that ever was or ever will be in the world.

With their ships already loaded, the merchants declared that they would not return home until they had seen Custance for themselves. Once they had seen her, they happily travelled back to Syria.

#

Aziz studied to become a civil engineer. He got married and his wife gave birth to five children. They travelled often. Aziz visited Great Britain four times before the war. He liked it a lot: a land of dignity, wealth, respect, democracy. Green. Some of his friends moved to the UK. Now that the civil war in Syria was entering its third year, Aziz was thinking about the island more often.

#

These merchants were much favoured by the Sultan of Syria. [...] Whenever they came back from any foreign place he invited them to be his guests and hungrily questioned them about the news from distant countries and wonders they had heard of or seen. Among other things the merchants told him about Lady Custance. They spoke of her beauty, of her nobility. They praised her so much, in such detail, that the Sultan felt a great desire to hold her in his arms. He wanted to love her for as long as he lived. [...]

'Without Custance,' he told his Council, 'I am as good as dead.'

The Council spoke at length about magic, about deception, but in the end they saw the only way to win her was to marry her. And then they understood the difficulties. There was such a difference between the laws of East and West. [...]

What need we say? There were treaties and embassies between the two realms. The Pope and the knights were all involved. [...] It was agreed that Custance would be accompanied on her journey by bishops, lords, ladies, knights of renown and other folk. […]

The Christian legation eventually arrived in Syria with a great solemn company.

Large was the crowd and rich the assembly of Syrians and Romans when they greeted each other. […]

Then the time arrived for the feast that the Sultaness had organised.

#

Daraa is a strategic city, crucial for defence of the capital, so the attacks of the Syrian Army and the counterattacks of the rebels became a daily occurrence.

'My whole family was against the regime,' Aziz says.

His speech becomes broken at times. A short outburst of words in Arabic is followed by a sudden silence. It sounds like automatic weapons in close combat. It sounds like the streets of his hometown today.

'In Daraa, under attack, everything became difficult,' Aziz says, and makes a very long pause. 'One of our children fell ill, and we couldn't find medicine in time. We have four children now.'

He holds his upper arms and rocks back and forth. Slow and steady, waves in the bay. I've seen this same movement, this same posture, in other times and other cultures. When the big emotional plates deep below the skin start hitting each other, this wave of pain appears on the surface.

'The Security found out it was me who reported occasionally for foreign media, and I was arrested. Twice.' He fires another short burst of memories and falls silent again. Waves.

This is the dark zone. I was asked not to ask about his imprisonment.

#

All the guests, Syrian and Christian, were cut or stabbed at the table. All of them cut into pieces, except Lady Custance. The old Sultaness, together with her henchmen, did it all. The old crone wanted to rule the country alone.

#

'My plan was to reach England,' Aziz says, 'but every country had closed the door in our face... I found a number and contacted a smuggler.

'The smuggler asked me to meet him in Skenderiye, in Egypt. When I arrived, he took me to a flat where there were a number of Syrians already. They were all waiting to leave.

'He promised us that the journey would start the same day, or the next one. It would be, he said, a half an hour trip by a fast boat to a bigger, very nice ship. The journey to Italy should take four to five days. It would cost €3,700.'

#

Custance was dragged to the port, put on a boat without a rudder, told to learn how to sail, and set on her way back to Italy.

#

'Nothing happened that day, or the next one. We remained hidden in that apartment. Suddenly, one night the smuggler came and said, "We are ready to leave." Small vans waited outside to take us to a village on a canal. I don't know where it was, but the water in the canal was in different colours and smelled of chemicals. They told me to lie low and covered me with something.

'After an hour, they took three of us into a fishing boat that was supposed to take us to a bigger ship. We spent two hours navigating through that canal.

'It was light enough to see the boat when we arrived to the sea. It was about 25 metres long. The boat was tied to a trawler and we were told this one would tug us to the big ship. There were armed people on the trawler. It was now too late to change my mind. I had no choice but to continue the journey.'

It was the 19th of May 2013.

#

Inauspicious ascent into oblique house! Unhappy Mars must have fallen out of his place into the darkest house of all. Oh feeble moon, unhappy your steps! You find yourself where you are not welcomed. Where you were well, from there you are driven away.

#

'There was no place to sleep, but at least for the first two days the weather was calm. Suddenly, the skies darkened, the wind howled, the sea turned on us. The rope that tied our boat to the trawler snapped. The captain said we couldn't continue. He said the trawler had mechanical problems and we had to go back to Skenderiye. We continued through the strong wind. Our boat was rocking dangerously. The captain promised we would get another boat from Libya.

'After two days the wind calmed down a little. The captain informed us there was no boat from Libya, but that we were now close to Italy. We didn't know where we were. It was already our sixth day on the sea. I had brought cheese and bread for five days, but managed to stretch it.'

#

For days, for years floated this creature across the eastern Mediterranean, and into the Strait of Gibraltar – such was her fate. Often she expected to die.

#

'We entered the Strait of Sicily close to Malta, and the captain said he went there for fishing. How, if the trawler really had problems? We sensed something bad was going on, as if it was a boat of death, so we demanded to go back to Egypt. We offered to pay him extra just to take us back. One of our party became desperate and threw himself overboard, but they went after him and saved him. At this stage we all threatened to throw ourselves into the sea. The captain stopped and turned the boat. He said we were going back and, in two days, we would be there.

'We were caught in another storm. We were out of food, and there was very little water. They gave us stale bread to eat, the one they used as bait, for fishing. It was very hard. We had to soak it in water to soften it.

'Then we saw the smuggler approaching on a new fishing boat, towing another boat behind. There were other passengers in it. Many of them. We were told this new trawler would take us to Italy.'

#

'Place her in the same ship in which she arrived here. […] Then push the ship out to sea. And forbid her ever to return.' Oh Custance, well may your spirit tremble. Well may your dreams be sorrowful.

#

'We were ordered into the new boat. Forty-four of us – men, women and children. The new boat was smaller than the old one. It didn't bode well. There was smoke coming from the engine room. Very dangerous. Behind us was the boat full of young Egyptians, we discovered. All under 18.

'Suddenly they moved all the Egyptians from the second boat to our boat, 75 of them, plus 44 of us. There was no place to move. The vessel was now too heavy, so the water came to the gunwales and started overflowing.

'Our original trawler turned and went back.

'The boat continued, but it was now very slow. Even though we had been told we were four hours away from Italy, they told us now there was at least 17 hours.

'The Egyptians told us about the plan: under the Italian laws anyone under the age of 18 could walk free, no detention at all. So they had informed the Italian Army to come and capture them. The Italians, they said, knew about us coming; they would wait for us.

'The night fell. We stood in the boat. There was no place to sit or lie down.

'Then it dawned and we couldn't see any other ship. We stood under the sun. There was no food.

'Another night. We stood in the boat. The water was overflowing.'

#

Since she was not slain at the feast, who kept her from drowning in the sea? Who saved Jonah in the belly of the whale until he was spat out at Nineveh? [...] It was a great miracle to feed the crowd of 5,000 only with five loaves and two fishes. [...]

Who saved her from drowning in the sea?

#

'Three ships of the Italian Coastguard arrived in the morning. But they didn't do anything, just surrounded our boat and stood like that, taking photos. I spoke to an Italian captain, I said, "Help us, the water is coming in, we are sinking." He said, "Tell us first the name of the smuggler." We said, "Help us, we are hungry, we don't have food or water." He said, "Give us the name." We refused to say the name. He said, "Then no food or water." I then gave them the names of three people I knew from Daraa, none of whom was the smuggler.

'They took us in. It was the 4th of June. My journey had taken 16 days.'

#

So she floated ahead into our own ocean and our own fierce northern seas. [...]

A victorious senator, sailing home to Rome, came upon the ship in which Custance was abandoned. Nothing he knew of who she was, or why in such state. She would not talk of her rank, ready to die but not reveal anything.

#

'They took us to the detention centre on Lampedusa.

'They lined us in a narrow corridor and told us they needed to get our fingerprints. The Egyptians knew the system: they gave their fingerprints right away and were let go. We Syrians asked, "Why do you need our fingerprints?" They said to check that we were not terrorists. But we had our ID cards, our passports... so we refused.

'For ten days we had no food, we were hungry, but we were told we wouldn't be given any food until we gave our fingerprints. We didn't want to do it because we all had our families back there, and the Italians would reveal that we were gone when checking with the Syrian Security.'

#

In her language, Custance asked for mercy, to be released from the misery of such life.

When he saw that there was nothing to find on the vessel, he brought the sad woman on to dry land. She kneeled down and thanked God for all the mercy. But who she was she would not tell anyone. Nothing good or bad would make her speak.

#

'The Italians took the women and children away and left us Syrian men in the corridor. Then came a police commander, whose face I will never forget. He ordered his men to beat us and they took our fingerprints by force.

'After that they gave us food and water.

'A woman from the UN Refugee Agency arrived. We told her about the beating, and she didn't believe us. After she checked with the Italian policemen and they confirmed our story, she came back and said, "It seems that this really happened, in which case you can go to court and state your case. But I don't think you would achieve anything. Better apply for asylum."

'Then she told us that for asylum they needed to take our fingerprints again. It was a separate process. We refused. They told us that in that case we had to go back to Syria. Some of my friends then agreed – gave their fingerprints and continued, some to Sweden, some to Germany, some to the UK, but I have a family, I went back to Syria. I thought, they beat us in Syria, they beat us in Italy – what's the difference?'

#

King Alla went to visit the home of the senator, and see the woman for himself. The senator greeted the king with great honours, and then sent after Custance. [...]

When Alla saw his wife, he greeted her gently and began

to weep so much it was hard to watch. He knew it was her. Custance herself, for sorrow, stood dumb as a tree. Her heart was shut. She swooned, then stood up, then swooned again. [...]

They wept together, lamented the past. Long was the sobbing and the bitter pain before their hearts could open again.

\#

'My family thought I was dead. It was the 19th of June when my mobile started working again. I was in Turkey. I called home and was told that my wife was arrested. She was accused of helping the insurgents. She is a nurse, of course it wasn't true. One of my brothers was also in jail.

'I entered Syria clandestinely. After some time they released my wife from prison. My brother was still in custody and my other brother was with the insurgents.'

\#

Who could describe the joy and sorrow that now filled the hearts of Custance, Alla and the Emperor? I shall make an end of this tale, the day is fading fast.

\#

'I couldn't stay in Syria. I went to another smuggler. He charged me €4,500 to take me by truck from Turkey to England. It was six of us, hidden behind some large boxes. Every night we would come out for some fresh air and to stretch out. Some of the passengers went to other countries, I don't know where. In the end I remained alone in the truck. I exited only when we were deep in the UK, in Nottingham. I was very ill by then. My kidney stone started hurting badly.

'When I arrived I called my friend who lives here to

come pick me up. In his apartment I recovered a few days, then I applied for asylum.

'I was put in a detention centre. I was very ill, and kept asking every single day to be released. It took them 100 days to let me go, in spite of the support of several organisations.'

#

And so in virtue and in charity they all lived. They were never parted, except by death itself. And farewell now. My tale has come to an end.

#

Aziz's story hasn't come to an end. His family is in Daraa and his wife is losing patience. He is now afraid that she would take their children and embark on one of the death boats.

Our talk is over. Aziz stands up to take the glass of water from the other table, and only now I realise that his clothes are the right size, but that he shrinks when he sits down, as if expecting a blow.

---

1. Excerpts from Geoffrey Chaucer's 'The Man of Law's Tale' as retold by the author.
2. Chaucer's spelling of 'Constance' – the names in this tale are as close to the originals as possible. Skenderiye, for example, is Alexandria.

The Chaplain's Tale

as told to

Michael Zand

inaudible words in into this world this anti world yes into this place like no no other but all around us yes and then he said for you my brothers yes for you yourselves are our letters brothers and you are written on our hearts you are known and read by everyone and then he sighed and took a long deep breath and said that in this dark in the dark in this darkness or if not exactly the dark then close enough to it there is a story and if not a story then a dance of an eagle and a fish and I a friend and servant of Christ Jesus by the will of God give to you God's holy people in this walled city a message of grace and peace in this walled place from our Father and from his many sons and daughters for you my brothers and for you my rays of light flash and fires flash and in into this world this anti world yes there a story of a man or in the dark any man who sighs and takes a long deep breath and the story yes in five acts and the first act is the sea and the second act is a deep guttural pain listen a deep guttural pain say nothing for just one a moment I said a deep guttural phh and the third act is words that are doubts that break stones can you imagine that there are doubts yes that's not difficult to imagine but there is stones and the stone is broken is loud enough to help us through my brothers and then the fourth act is a cave and is nothing to do more importantly the cave is nothing to do with any art and the fifth act which should be the final act is an intermittent beauty and the sea brother the sea mmm again mmm again yes this is the story of a man marked by a series of haunting sounds from his childhood and these sounds that he heard and understood but whose meaning he was to forget these sounds are yes these are sounds that he heard on one particular occasion these are sounds that he heard when he witnessed the yes very good you see there is a line and the line is drawn with the end of a stick on the ground or whatever passes for the ground at the time so yes you see a line is drawn with a stick on the ground and on a winter afternoon on a hill outside another church similar to this yes or you see it on a particularly warm night crowds gathering after a storm yes well whatever in the early morning in a field where a cockerel sits weighting weighting you see you see you see it was something and so afterwards he returned home yes to a place thousands of miles from there thousand nights from listen say nothing for just one a moment thousands miles from mmm the sea in the his own language in the laws of his language in the mmm mmm and soon soon

afterwards the world closed in around him yes the meaning of that night faded you see it was deaded and and many wrote and spoke with wit and some fancied themselves as poets or archaeologists and a few even tried to venture beyond digging through the layers mining under the earth slipping back and avoiding outcomes drowned in the glory of their own fragments until disgust until disgust until they asked the women and the girls to walk to the bottom of the hill and they asked him to send down his son too but he refused you see because he wanted to be with him and then they all they they deep guttural pain and deep guttural pain and a pause and deep guttural pain and head bowed and a pause and inaudible words and yes drums and shibboleths and shibboleths and drums and shibboleths and shibboleths and drums shibboleths drums in comprehensible yes and the they found him in the hinterland searching for some half meanings in the confusion and disorder of his broken words and sounds and yes he had a new language and this was his only language because it was the only language he could now trust was you see very good because outside his brothers outside of the walls he could hear someone he didn't know who was breaking stones and the more he touched the walls around him the more he realised how ordinary they were as if they were built to match a pencil sketch a small child might do if he were told to draw walls and he said the guards tell me they are surfaces membranes between us and he said I hope they are I hope so I hope they are because if they are if they are between us then they makes us us because they make us us and he learnt to write his poetry on the walls in the hope that his brothers on the outside would see it and take notice until one day he realised what the noise was he was hearing the drilling of his cave he was hearing his brothers on the outside breaking its stone sides rrrr and the like the like of these children of God that he knew they were they had seen his words and he had seen them in his dreams and they had all begun to doubt the lies that they had been told drums and shibboleths and the stone walls and the necessity of language and he could hear his fellow brothers on the outside because they were breaking prejudice with chisels and hammers and drills they were breaking through ground work rrrr and even around the walls around him where the world was strong and hard he could and they would tremble with the sounds of chisels and hammers and drills rrrr yes and long after in a sudden

flash suddenly and gradually he realised that this this cave is nothing to do with any art nnn and long after in a sudden flash suddenly and gradually he realised the longer he stayed within its confines nnn the more he realised that his cave had nothing to do with art the playful practice of art or even the illustrated memoirs of art but instead it offered a constant drone a constant repetitive a dulling of the a contraction of the a distraction by the whoever whatever nnnn and after at first in a sudden flash

suddenly gradually he equated this noise to madness nnnn in
the brain in the ears in the electric discharge from his fingertips
and his stories not torture as such but constant and repetitive
listless nonexistence procrastination of the social dynamic but in
time over a period of many he learned to harness its energy
however ridiculous it sounds he realised that the walls of his
cave had their own resonance their own frequency it had the
capability to takes his particular experience and freeze its
meaning and to transform it into pure form he had discovered
the substances and forces that keep us human and extend the
warmth of any place even his place of perpetual incarceration
throughout the universe he had become yes very good he had
become an exhalation of intermittent beauty you see that's the
nub of it my brothers it's a beauty yes but an intermittent
beauty of sorts forged by the pain of Christ Jesus by the will of
God so you see you see the beauty of this story is in two parts
and you see there are some parallels and a few empathies
between them you feel part of one and part of both and you
may well if you have blood in your veins and yes that one leads
directly to the other yes that means you have power yes that you
can make rational conjunctions and that you can
compartmentalise the sounds and their connotations and the
mind thus casts out and renounces the rich and ample matter
of all thoughts and restricts itself to the poverty of a single
sequence of sounds is is which means we need to think again
we need to think in a different way where the energy runs but
not against any one person or any one thing because the surge
exists and fountains and there will always be sounds we cannot
understand or remember but that are still essential confusing
beautiful that still encourage us to start again because one day
thaa they will come for him yes they will come to the cave and
he will have gone and they will know who he is and pause and
he will be with us or he will be with us again maranatha in into
this world this this anti world of of inaudible words

The Unaccompanied Minor's Tale

as told to

Inua Ellams[3]

SENEBESH IS HOLDING DANI'S hand under the rusting jeep in a car park in Khartoum. She is trying to stifle the laughter which is as ripe as fruit in her mouth. It is leaking out of the corners of her lips and, if she lets it burst, the consequences would be disastrous.

Moments before, Dani gave in to Senebesh's request. 'Tell me a funny story,' she'd asked and Dani cleared his throat. 'One day, an Arab couple went on a romantic honeymoon to London...' 'I like this story,' Senebesh interrupted. 'Shush! Let me talk!' Dani continued: 'The wife barely spoke English. When they got to the hotel, the receptionist told them: "Anything you want, just call, I'm here." In the evening, when the husband had gone to buy food, a mouse ran across the floor and the wife started screaming. "Hello! Hello!" She had called the reception. "What is it?" the man asked. The wife didn't know the word so asked, "You know *Tom and Jerry*, the cartoon?" "Yes," said the man, "Jerry not Tom, Jerry is here!"'

Years from now, when you ask Senebesh what it was like, the smile that will ghost her lips is this fruit of a memory, this singular joy, but it will fade to something dark.

Senebesh met Dani at the camp in Gedaref a few months before, and saw the 14-year-old kid beneath his rehearsed swagger. He harshly demanded water and, when she frowned at him through the cloud of dust, he asked politely. She laughed as he guzzled loudly, his throat like a drain pipe. When he finished, he asked if she'd like to hear a story and kept Senebesh entertained for a solid hour. Ever since, she'd seek him out for more. Dani was safe, charming, but Abbas was the wild one.

Under the rusting Jeep they could hear the approaching Sudanese Police, their boots scuffing earth. 'Come out! We know you are here!' Senebesh pressed her full mouth to the ground as Dani whispered, 'Jerry! Jerry!' And when she felt she could hold it no longer, they heard Abbas yelling: 'Don't you have bigger thieves to catch? Useless police! You want something to do? Catch me if you can…' and ran as they gave chase. 'Told you! He is never late!' Dani said as Senebesh brushed dust off herself and turned towards the market in Khartoum. 'Just a fist full of dollars more,' Dani said, quoting a favourite film, 'then tomorrow we leave for Libya.'

Abbas had organised everything. He was a year older than Senebesh, but streets, decades smarter. He planned their escape from the camp, promising: 'No more queues for stale bread, no more denim-jean tents, no more bathing in the river, no more diarrhoea-ridden food… come with me, we'll cross the desert together! Us against the world!' 'Three musketeers?' Dani asked, his eyes brightening, 'Yes!' Abbas added: '…whoever they are.' They were a fantastically effective team, swapping shifts, washing dishes in kitchens, cleaning taxis, selling fabric, fruit… anything they could lift in the Khartoum heat, they'd hawk, whilst Abbas kept the police at bay: succumbing to their demands for bribes, cursing when they wanted more, using them to ward off rough smugglers who bullied, demanding large fees to arrange their journey through the Sahara. All this was a full-time job and Dani was thankful Abbas was up to it.

Months from now, in the desert night, when Abbas is pouring petrol in their bottled water to stop them gulping, to make the water last, Dani will have to remind himself of Abbas' good intentions. He will have to have faith.

Senebesh loved the camp in Gedaref. Years from now, in the loneliness of English streets, she will miss its community, the togetherness of suffering, how even when the police and thieves returned the women they'd kidnapped, brought them back bleeding, swollen, a rag between their thighs, the camp would heal her and revenge together. The night she was almost taken, she found the boys and handed over her savings. 'Three musketeers,' she said. Abbas asked why she'd left Eritrea, though he knew the reason. It was the same for so many: faith. Only Orthodox Islam and Christianity were allowed in Eritrea. Her family, secret Pentecostal Christians, held gatherings for others till a neighbour informed the Eritrean Police. The house was raided, her father imprisoned, mother killed, sister vanished, the house burned and a warrant issued for her arrest. So Senebesh left. When Abbas asked Dani why he had left, he explained he didn't want to join the Eritrean Army. His older brothers and father had died in its compulsory service and he chose to live. When they asked Abbas his reasons for wanting to leave Sudan, he laughed into the night's slow breeze. 'Next time,' he said. 'But tomorrow we go to Khartoum. After two months, Libya. My sister...' he said to Senebesh, 'you cannot stay here any more.'

1/ Lip balm for Senebesh. 2/ Gloves for cold nights. 3/ Goggles for the sand storms. 4/ A bottle of fuel. 5/ A fast driver... Abbas, who had found the driver with the best reputation, who gathered the provisions for the month-long crossing, rolled off another list: 'Rules For Survival,' he whispered as they boarded the truck. 1/ People go mad in the desert. Trust no one. 2/ Eighty-eight people to each jumbo truck. 3/ Most will sit on top of the roof. 4/ If you fall asleep you will fall off. Don't sleep. 5/ If you are in the middle, you will fight other passengers. 6/ All drivers are vagabonds with guns. They take women and do what they want. 7/ The best seat is on the outside, by the driver's window. 8/ The journey will feel like an incredible film, but if you die, you won't come back. 9/ Find a good God to believe in. 10/ It is always longer than you think.

Six weeks from now, in Zuwara in Libya, waiting to cross the sea to Italy, Dani will question what Abbas did. Senebesh will explain his sacrifice, Dani won't understand. Senebesh will compile her own list. It will become a mantra. She'll say to him, 'This is what happened':

1/ There was no GPS. 2/ The truck got lost in the deep of the desert. 3/ The third time it broke down, the men had to push. 4/ The driver drove off when the engine kicked in leaving some men behind. 5/ The fourth time it stopped, Abbas refused to push. 6/ The driver wanted the truck lighter. 7/ The driver wished to ditch an old woman. 8/ Abbas fought to keep her on. 9/ The driver wanted Senebesh. 10/ The driver kicked Dani's water. 11/ The driver told Abbas to choose. 12/ Abbas could not, so chose himself. 'Save your tears sister, you need the water,' he said and waved until they vanished, a dot among the dunes.

★

'Tell me a story,' Senebesh begged. The truck had just arrived in Tripoli and Dani was in a daze. Senebesh couldn't tell if he was seeing the dozens of bodies they'd passed in the desert, the flies harvesting their rotting flesh, or if he was hypnotised by the tap, by water. They'd watched three people die of thirst on the truck, listened to others wailing in the night, hallucinating, asking for beers and cold drinks before a silence claimed them. He stood by the tap, sipping and instantly refilling his bottle, refusing to move, guarding each drop, unable to believe such a thing could be free again. Senebesh gently took the bottle from his hands. 'Dani, story!' Dani blinked for several seconds trying to concentrate. 'Okay,' he said. 'There was a poor boy who used to pass under a tree by a stream and throw stones at the fruit. When they fell, he would eat the juicy oranges.

'One day, he found a wall built on the road, the tree was on the other side and a man stood guarding it. The boy begged the man to give him a fruit, but he refused, cursing the boy. Desperate, the boy threw stones hoping the man would simply catch a falling fruit and throw it over, but the man would eat the fruit and throw the stones back at the boy. So, the boy had an idea. He threw a large stone but made sure to miss, so, though it almost hit him, it rolled into the stream. The man was so angry, he grabbed an orange and threw it, which the boy caught, said, "Thank you," and ran away eating, laughing, eating and laughing,' Dani said, laughing at his own story. 'Thank you,' Senebesh said, silently also thanking God that Dani had found a glimmer of his old self. 'Are you hungry?' she asked.

They ate a fried chicken (a whole one each) on the journey from Tripoli to the fishing port of Zuwara, marvelling at each hot morsel, chewing slowly, softly, deliberately. Of the 88 they left with, 19 died or were left in the desert. Eight Nigerians, nine Ghanaians, three Ivorians, 11 Syrians and other Eritreans survived. Some had lost uncles, brothers, sisters, even their children crossing the desert and those who made it to the end, Senebesh made sure to remember. She knew them by name, weeping as she said goodbye. Aliyah, who'd lost her daughter crossing, wept too, unconsolably, refusing to leave Senebesh. 'My brother went before me, he is in Lampedusa, I just have to get to him.' 'But you don't yet have the money to cross,' Senebesh said. 'There are easy ways,' she replied, looked to the ground, flicked her eyes at the group of sea smugglers huddled together, looking at her hungrily, then stared back into Senebesh's wide face. Senebesh looked away, understanding what she meant. Aliyah made enough in four days. The others would have to work for months in Libya, sleeping in warehouses on the harbour, beyond which lay Lampedusa, the island-prison in Italy, the place the refugees are held, the first stop in Europe.

★

'They call it the blue desert you know,' Dani said sitting down heavily, waking Senebesh up. 'Another desert?' she shouted over the boat's engine. 'It is just as hot, nothing grows and it's endless.' 'How long left?' 'Sixty-two hours,' Dani replied. 'We've only been sailing for ten?' Dani shrugged as Senebesh turned to find the Libyan shore, now a barely visible strip in the distance. Of the 430 people crammed onto the inflatable boat, a stern-looking Senegalese man, the unofficial captain, barked at her, 'Look for oil rig, we're not going back to Libya, don't look back.' Senebesh glanced at the satellite phone and GPS tracker in his hand. After basic lessons in steering, the smugglers gave these to him, told him to sail for an oil rig near Lampedusa, that the workers would alert the Italian coastguards, that the plan isn't to reach the island, but to be rescued, and the boats were designed so. 'What you looking at?' the captain barked again. 'Nothing,' Senebesh said, as Dani moved to stand between them, fixing the man with a hard stare. 'Leave her alone! You've bigger things to worry about!' 'What things?' Senebesh whispered, and her face fell as Dani explained. 'We are too many for this boat. It's held together with glue, the smugglers use anything. The glue is melting. The man over there spread his water-soaked jacket over the melting part, has to splash water on it, keep it wet in all this heat.' 'Will it hold for long?' she asked. 'Two days, no more...' That's not enough time!' 'That's why he is nervous,' Dani said. 'The coastguards are our only hope.'

Senebesh didn't sleep that night. She couldn't. She counted stars over the Mediterranean, matched her breathing with the snoozing others, nibbled at her ration of biscuits and dried injera, and whenever she remembered, splashed sea water on the jacket even though it was too cold for the glue to melt anyway. She became the jacket's sole guardian, watching over it, a hawk in the blue desert. On the third day, when too many holes had appeared, when the boat began to sink, when the weak engine started struggling, dolphins appeared on either side and in front, keeping pace with the boat, leaping in and out of the water, playing as they chugged towards Lampedusa. Dani would remember them for the rest of his life; he thought of them as water angels, a sign things would be alright, thinking this just as Italian coastguards arrived, circled their boat, barked at them harshly in Italian, spoke into their radios and sped off again. The waves rocked their frail boat and overwhelmed the engine. It stuttered out just as Aliyah found her brother.

At first they thought they were items of clothing, cast-offs from others who crossed, but the closer they got, the clearer they saw that caged among the fabric, some stiff, some swollen, were the water-drenched flesh of refugees like them. They recoiled as one, all tried to turn away from the bodies but couldn't. They began to make out faces. Some looked serene, peaceful, asleep, as if, if Senebesh reached out to prod, they'd wake gently. Some had holes for eyes where the fish had feasted, others had fingers nibbled to the bone or torn off completely and the closer they got to Lampedusa, the more bodies their boat bumped into. With each wet thud, each body, each drowned flesh slapping against the boat, the people flinched. The dolphins had vanished now, and as Aliyah looked, fearing the worst, she saw her brother floating, his eyes intact, staring upwards, dead to the sky. She dived in after him. The others screamed at her to come back in. Senebesh tried to lunge after her but Dani caught her in time. In the commotion, the boat began to rock, more sea water seeping in, sinking the boat faster till they were submerged in the wide open sea. In the distance, they heard the Italian coastguards' sirens with larger boats in tow and struck out towards them, swimming best as they could, gurgling, swallowing and spitting out sea water, thrashing in the blue desert.

Two hours from now, on Lampedusa, Senebesh will watch the captain standing motionless in shock. Aliyah will be holding on to her brother's corpse. Senebesh will search among the survivors and find Dani gone. The coastguards will shake their heads when she asks if there are more and she will lose her appetite, she won't eat at all.

---

3. 'The Unaccompanied Minor's Tale' was generated from a series of improvisation, storytelling and character-generation workshops with groups of unaccompanied minors living in Canterbury.

The Lorry Driver's Tale

as told to

Chris Cleave

WE AREN'T AT ALL like you. They keep us apart, for your protection. There'll be a blue sign at the entrance to any ferry port or motorway services: you take this lane and we'll take that. Fifty feet on there'll be red-and-white MarroBar between the lanes, in case you have a last-minute change of allegiance. You won't, though. You'll keep right, our lane will turn left, and you'll never think of us again. In your life you'll have more conversations with optimists and murderers than you will with lorry drivers.

And yet there are more of us than there are of farmers, police and teachers combined. Our average age is 53. We're male, and white, and we have bad backs. We're twice as likely as you to be divorced or separated. But we don't ask for your sympathy. Read the stickers: all we ask is for your cyclists not to pass us on the inside. There are 700,000 goods vehicle drivers in Britain and we are all self-medicating with bacon rolls. We're three per cent of the workforce, 20 per cent of the studio audience for *Top Gear*, and 40 per cent of the petition to have it put back on TV. They say we're the core of the UKIP vote, but they shouldn't take us for granted. As the lorry driver said to the politician: if you can't see my mirrors, I can't see you.

When it comes to illegals, we know what the media won't tell you. We catch them sneaking round the back of our

25

trailers. We find them crawling behind the cartons in the load. You probably know the global economic push factors or whatever, but we know how they smell. We're the ones who have to drag them out of the space above the axles. They're in the shadows whenever we turn our back – it's like a horror film. As long as their country is a nightmare and ours is a dream, they'll come in the night. But you're the ones who are sleepwalking.

On this one trip I'll tell you about, I was doubling with another driver and we were homeward bound through Calais. If immigration is a horror film then Calais is the scene where the zombies are massing. You see them out of the corner of your eye at first, when you're still a couple of hundred kilometres out. Say you're pulling in to Saint-Quentin for diesel. You give them the hard eye and they act casual, hands in their pockets – but no one's fooled. Because they're Somali and Rwandan zombies, not Parisian zombies with berets and baguettes. A blind lefty could pick them out of a line up.

The illegals can pick out the lefties, too. They're the ones driving home from a little place with lavender and wi-fi. They always call it a 'little place'. If it was their own lady parts they were referring to, they couldn't be more coy. They keep to their side of the services, topping up their tanks while the euro is so weak. They think the illegals should be allowed in, but when they say 'in', they don't mean *in their car*. It would be easy to do – it's not as if the Border Force ever look in the boot of a family motor – but that isn't how liberals think. They're intellectually fearless, rather than actually brave.

So the zombies creep towards our lorries instead. We'll be in Saint-Quentin, filling up, and all the time we've got one eye on the pump and the other on the illegals. Take your eye off and they'll sidle up to the trailer and do the stupid stuff they do. As if we're not going to look in the back before we get to the ferry port. As if we're not going to go up on the gantry and find them clinging on, and tell them to eff off. If there's one English phrase they're going to learn, it's that. I feel sorry for them, for what it's worth. They're desperate and they're not very bright and I know this because there are three easier ways of getting across the Channel than stowing away in an HGV.

On this one trip I'm telling you about, we were double manning, as I say, and so my co-driver – I'll call him Mr Hyde because he's yellowish and rough – he could stand on the other side of the trailer and shoo the illegals away while I filled up the diesel. And on this trip we had a journalist along too. I'll call him Clark Kent but you know his name – he's famous for slagging off restaurants. And once every six months he writes about a burning social issue so people won't start thinking: hang on, you're just a tiring man who doesn't enjoy eating out anymore.

I suppose the six months had come up on his tachograph because here he was, sitting up in the cab, dropping his aitches to make us feel at home. The boss had said to be nice to him. She'd given me 500 extra in cash, with a warning that she'd take it back off my wages if the famous man didn't have a nice day. The 500 was still in its manila envelope, safely tucked under my seat.

Once I'd done the diesel fill I climbed into the cab. Clark Kent had set up a webcam on the dashboard because apparently he was live-streaming the whole thing. Mr Hyde didn't want to be in the shot, so the camera was just on me and Clark. It sat there on the dashboard like the unblinking Eye of Islington.

'So what do these buttons do?' Clark was saying. 'Do you have alarms and whatnot?'

'Those are the temp dials for the trailer. That one turns on the stereo.'

'Oh, do you listen to music?'

I wondered what he thought we might listen to – the speeches of Enoch Powell – but the camera was on so I just said, 'Yeah, whatever's on the radio.'

'Mind if I twiddle?'

'Be my guest.'

'I haven't used one of these things for years,' said Clark,

prodding away. (I honestly don't know what he meant. His fingers, maybe.)

He found Autoroute FM, which does bad French songs on a playlist, and he thought it very droll. We all laughed about it. It was hilarious that foreigners had radio stations featuring hits of the 60s, 70s and 80s. We rolled on towards Calais.

'You don't talk much,' said Clark to Mr Hyde.

In fact I'd told him not to talk, because I knew how that would end.

'He's just tired,' I said. 'He was on until we picked you up in Reims.'

'You take the driving in turns, do you?'

'No,' I said, 'we take Benzedrine and fondle each other to stay awake.'

Actually I said, 'Yeah, in the EU it's four-and-a-half hours each, then switch. We have a digi-card that keeps track of our hours.'

'It must get tiring.'

'No worse than journalism, I suppose. You have deadlines, don't you?'

'Tell me about it. Before I came out for this trip I had to do a Michelin-starred place in Maidstone. It was utterly bogus, and then I had to write it up on the ferry. I couldn't work out if I was furious or seasick.'

'Still,' I said, 'I'd swap with you.'

'You say that, but there are only so many menus a man can read before he wonders if this is really his life's main course.'

I wondered if he talked like that when the cameras weren't on. I had a flash of what it would be like being married to him. I was exhausted already, and we'd only just met.

We reached the turn-off for Arras, which is where the zombie menace starts to be obvious. There was a bunch of them lurking on the slip road, all bones and nylon parkas.

'Christ,' said Clark. 'You weren't joking.'

'No one believes it until they see with their own eyes. It's a plague.'

Clark talked to the webcam. 'I can see one or two dozen dark-skinned males, loitering by the exit from these services.'

'More like three or four dozen,' I said. 'There'll be more of them hiding behind that toilet block.'

'Do you feel sympathy?'

'We can't, can we? It's us who get punished when one of them stows away. We get an eight grand fine. Two strikes and we lose our licence.'

'Still, they're human beings. Don't you feel compassion?'

He gave me the same look as when he'd seen my UKIP flag on the back wall of the cab – as if I wasn't necessarily evil, but that I couldn't be expected to know any better.

'I have to think of my career,' I said. 'I'm in it for the long haul.'

He laughed, at least. 'But seriously, don't you feel any empathy?'

'Do you? When one of your reviews shuts down an eatery?'

'That's different though, isn't it? No one forces a Michelin chef to serve me a flightless vol-au-vent.'

Mr Hyde scowled at him and said in his Italian accent, 'No one forces these scum to hide in my lorry.'

Clark turned to look at him. 'I feel like we haven't met.'

I laughed to calm things down. 'Ignore him, his mother's an I-Tie – he's practically an immigrant himself.'

'I'm a racist,' said Mr Hyde. 'There. Put that in your bloody newspaper. I hate illegals because I love the UK.'

I shushed him. 'He means that if it was your mother the illegals were moving in next door to, you'd see it differently. If your kids couldn't get a flat because immigrants get higher on the housing list, you'd be sick of it.'

'Then you're complaining about a social housing shortage, aren't you, not an immigration crisis.'

'You say potato.'

'Actually I say croquette of heritage King Edwards à l'hollandaise, and I wouldn't mind if these people made a new life next door to me.'

Mr Hyde opened his mouth but I shot him a look to shut up.

'Please,' I said, 'you're in the wrong lorry if you want to talk about the philosophy of it all. All we can do is show you what it's really like out here on the frontline, and your readers can make up their own minds.'

'Alright, fair enough. Then I think my first question would be: how do the stowaways make it through, if you're always checking your lorries?'

'Some drivers are careless, aren't they? Me, I won't stop within a hundred kilometres of Calais, but there's always some Charlie who lets his hours expire and has to pull over. By the end of your statutory break, you'll have illegals in your load, in your wheel arches, in your engine compartment. You'd be amazed at the gaps they squeeze into.'

'Don't the border guys find them? They have scanners, no?'

'They're only human. Zombies will always get through if they're well-enough hidden. And some of the drivers, for a fee, have ways of hiding them.'

'Really? There are drivers who'd risk that?'

I had to smile. 'Listen, what do you make in a year?'

He winked at the camera. 'I make 52 Saturdays less dull.'

'Well I make 28k, with an ex and a current and four teenage kids. If I was unpatriotic, I could triple my money. Not all illegals are skint, you know.'

'Are you serious?'

'The situation is what's serious. Ever since the Trojan horse, there's been people smuggling. Ever since Han Solo took Obi Wan Kenobi's money, in a galaxy far, far away.'

'I'm warming to our chauffeur,' said Clark to the camera. 'I came expecting that a lorry driver would be unreconstructed, but maybe there's more to this profession than I gave it credit for. Have your say by using the hashtag *#stowaways*.'

We drove through the outskirts of Calais. I pulled into the HGV lane and we joined the queue for the ferry port. In their own lanes the normals rolled past, refugees from their little places. Behind the glass you could see their lips moving as they argued whether there would have been time to stop at the last supermarket, to stock up on saucisson and those French school exercise books, the ones with the graph paper pages.

Clark said, 'What would you do, if you found someone in the back of this lorry right now? What would you say to them?'

'Well for a start I'd need to scrape the Brie off them. We're carrying eighteen thousand kilos of it.'

'But seriously?'

'Seriously?' I put my hand over the webcam, making sure to cover the mic as well as the lens. 'The two of us would drag him out and give him a kicking. Because *one*, the load would be contaminated and the company would have to write off a hundred grand. And *two*, you need to get the word out that you don't mess with British lorries. An old-fashioned kicking sends that message in every language the illegals speak.'

'God! Have you ever done that?'

'All of us have done it. It's standard.'

I took my hand off the webcam and he said into it, 'Our driver has just told me something profoundly shocking about what happens to stowaways if they're discovered.'

'Your readers should try being out here before they judge us.'

He looked into the camera again. 'Now I don't even know what I expected. I thought we'd found some common ground, but I have to say I'm shocked and disappointed. It's as if these lorries have space for 40 tonnes of cargo but no room for basic humanity.'

'Nice. Did you write that one before you came out?'

Now he put his own hand over the camera. 'Look, don't take it personally. You show up with your UKIP flag and talk about beating up the little man, of course I'm going to make you look like a dick. What did you think? I'm doing my job, same as you.'

It was awkward after that, in the cab. At the end of the Customs queue I stopped the lorry and it made those hissing, sighing noises – as though it was powered by sadness under unbelievable pressure. The Border Force people put their scanners over the load and then gave us the manual checks, starting at the back of the trailer and working their way forward to the cab. When they saw Clark Kent it was like Christmas for them. In their commando jumpers, bless – they couldn't get enough of him. And in fairness he was a gentleman – he signed autographs, and posed for selfies, and turned the webcam round to live stream them. They mugged for the camera and they weren't even bothered with our passports – we could have travelled on our library cards.

Afterwards on the ferry, Clark seemed subdued. The fans had been spun sugar for him, and we were kryptonite. We took him to the lorry drivers' lounge, away from the hoi-polloi, and I even bought him a coffee and a Chelsea bun. I wondered if he was going to review it, but he only set up his phone to film us, then sipped his drink and stared out at the waves.

'Cheer up,' I said. 'You'll never have to see us again after Dover.'

'There is that, I suppose.'

'Then why the long face? Do you have a terrine that you're overdue to be angry about?'

'It's just that I feel so sorry for them. They're so thin, aren't they? And their eyes, when they were waiting on that slip road. Just so absolutely despairing. Imagine not being allowed into the country.'

'Imagine *having* to come into the country, though. Imagine having to drop off 90,000 rounds of brie and drive home to Ruislip in the rain. Imagine having to read your restaurant reviews every Saturday morning.'

'That's life though, isn't it? Turns out people will cling on to your axles for a chance at it.'

'I suppose I'm just used to seeing them.'

'Well I'm not. Seeing them desperate for what we have, it makes you realise what we've got.'

'There you go – you've taken the first step. The next is to admit they'll destroy what we have unless we keep them out.'

He shook his head. 'I won't ever take that step. That's the difference between you and me, I suppose.'

'We're different, I'll give you that.'

We looked out together through the scratched Perspex windows. I've never got why people like the sea. It's cold and unreliable. On dry land it would be a cat or an economist. Luckily we were almost into Dover already – it's barely a ditch, the English Channel. If I was an illegal I'd rent a pedallo.

'Is there any ground we haven't covered today?' said Clark. 'Anything you'd like to say that you haven't had the chance to?'

'Just that I hope this has let people see what it's really like. Out here we're simple people, operating on the simple facts, and the fact is we can't be having stowaways.'

'Well, thank you for your time,' said Clark, turning off the camera on his phone.

The three of us went to the lorry deck, down through the layers of car drivers to where the real business of the day was parked. While we waited to disembark, I made Clark pack away the webcam. When the ramp came down, we rolled out through the port. There was a chippie van in the first layby – *First Plaice* – and I pulled in because it was late and we hadn't eaten.

I sent Mr Hyde down to fetch us all fish and chips. I gave him the manila envelope of cash from under my seat. I told him to keep the change. He shook my hand and that was it – he was gone. I watched him disappear in the off-side wing mirror. I watched until he was just a speck – just a germ – although it's worth bearing in mind that objects in the mirror are closer than they appear.

The layby was quiet. A few seagulls stalked about, stabbing in the dust for old chips. You could see the white cliffs over the roofs of the warehouse buildings. In fairness, they're off-white.

After five full minutes, Clark Kent finally got it. 'He's not coming back, is he?'

'Not unless he gets homesick and wants us to take him on the return trip.'

Clark began laughing and shaking his head. 'My God.'

'You write one word about this and I'll swear you were in on it.'

'Right. Of course. But I mean… Christ. Do you know where he's from?'

'Syria. Most of them can pass for Italian. I'll only take them if they've got convincing papers.'

He said nothing, only shook his head and looked out at the gulls.

'You know what?' he said after a while. 'I haven't had fish and chips for I don't know how long.'

We got cod-and-large times two and leaned against the bumper to eat them. I splashed vinegar on mine. Clark drizzled it on his. He sniffed the bottle and winced. The seagulls made those calls they make, of dead souls mocking the living.

'How many times have you done this?'

'Enough.'

'Do they pay you for it?'

I shook my head. 'Don't take it personally, but you're the first passenger I've taken a fee for.'

'So why do you do it?'

'It's the kick, isn't it? To be different inside. Last freedom we've got.'

'What made you start?'

'Like you said, it's different once you've seen their eyes. You realise if they can carry all that, maybe you can take some of the load. You might as well help – life's over so fast.'

'It's a short trip in a long vehicle.'

I sighed. 'You do write this stuff in advance.'

'It was going to be my title for the piece.'

The gulls went up a gear, distraught at all their liberty.

'How are your fish and chips?' I said.

He frowned at his Styrofoam tray. 'Fine,' he said. 'A little rustic.'

The Arriver's Tale

as told to

Abdulrazak Gurnah

I CAME BY AIR. It may sound odd to say that – what other way then? Some people walked. Many drowned. They were desperate. I wasn't desperate but I was very frightened because I had made some people very angry with me. My crime was to tell the girls who attended my Sunday school that they should not agree to be circumcised. My Sunday school was supposed to be a reading and writing class but I slipped in the good word any way I could. I told them circumcision was genital mutilation and a barbaric and backward practice. Men forced women to do it so they would know they were rubbish. The real intention was to hurt them and paralyse them and control them. When the day came for the girls to agree to the cut, six of them refused. I wasn't there, but I discovered what had happened that same night when I heard angry voices outside my house, bidding me to come out and take a beating for interfering with their daughters. It was a Muslim village in a Muslim country, and though I am a countryman, I'm a Christian who was now accused of interfering with their daughters. You can imagine my terror.

When it quietened down outside and the angry people went away, perhaps to get more people to come and help them, I wheeled out my bicycle in the dark and rode away to safety in a nearby village. The next day I heard that the thatch of my house was set on fire that night and that the people

35

who did it were still looking for me and talking bad, so I ran away to the city, to the office of the charity NGO I worked for. The officer there was an Englishman, Bernard, he was my friend. He told me he would find out about the fire, that I shouldn't worry, everything will be all right, but I thought I would go into hiding. A few days later he told me that the people who burnt down my house came to look for me at the office, and they said they had some unfinished business with me. He told me to go the police. That made me laugh. I did not mean to laugh, it just came out of me. I told Bernard the police will beat me first and then hand me over to their brothers to finish the job. In that case you have no choice but to stay in hiding because those men looked dangerous. These bad people went back to the office several times looking for me, and in the end Bernard suggested that I run away to Britain to seek asylum. It is a Christian country, and you are a Christian worker persecuted for doing Christian labour, Bernard said. He knew I would be given sanctuary, he said. Bernard himself was leaving, and he gave me his telephone number in London in case I needed him.

How did I find the money for the fare? Friends helped me. My relatives promised to take care of my family. They could all see that my life was in danger, and this one spoke to that one until a fare for an Air Morocco flight to London was found. Friends arranged it all. So then I came by air, as I have already told you, and I arrived in London not knowing right from left, confused by the large spaces and the hushed crowds. But I talked myself into feeling strong, telling myself that I was doing something brave. I was wearing a suit I had made before I left and which I still have and wear on special occasions, so I also told myself I was looking good. I was given some forms to complete and I wrote what was necessary to save a life and I was allowed to enter, I don't know how. I was confused and didn't know right from left, but somehow I said what was needed, because I knew they would not turn me away. I was persecuted for doing merciful labour and I knew that London would not turn me away.

I rang the number Bernard gave me and he was happy to hear from me but he said I could not go and stay with him. His wife said no. He said maybe we could meet somewhere for a coffee after I had settled down. I sat there in the airport not knowing what to do next. Then a policeman approached me and suggested I go upstairs because it was warmer there. He asked me if I was all right, if I needed help. I wanted to tell him that I had nowhere to stay, that I only had a little money but I thought he had taken me for a respectable person and if I spoke to him like that he would think I was just an African hooligan. So I went upstairs and did not ask for his help.

I rang a friend from home who was living in Colchester. I am in London, I told him.

That's brilliant news, he said.

I'm coming to see you, I told him.

Wonderful, he said.

I don't have any money, I told him. He sent me the fare by Western Union and that same evening I was in Colchester with my friend and his family. My friend teased me about my smart suit and we laughed to see each other again after so long, but even as I ate the food his wife prepared for me, he told me I could not stay with them. I had already seen that myself. Him and his wife and their three small children lived in a small flat with only two rooms, and everything that I saw in their house told me that their lives were a struggle.

No, he said, now that I had arrived I must go to the Home Office and ask for asylum. So he gave me the money and the next day I went to Croydon, yes, to Lunar House. No, I was not frightened, maybe a little anxious because I did not want to get lost and make a fool of myself. There at Lunar House, a woman interviewed me and wrote down all my details. I told her that I was a campaigner against female genital mutilation and my life was in danger in my home country.

Yes, she said, I am going to assign you emergency initial accommodation, just sit there and wait now.

By the end of the day there were six of us waiting there and we were all put in a van and taken to Barry House. There were 12 of us there, and we could go out if we wanted to. Mostly I walked up and down the road, and if anyone looked in my direction I smiled to show my gratitude for the welcome their country had given me. I stayed there for five days. We told each other stories of our escape from danger and death. Then three of us were sent to live in a house in Newcastle where we stayed for a month. Then after that I was given a flat in Glasgow and three weeks' money, and all this time I was still waiting to be interviewed so that I could explain my need for sanctuary. I was eager for my interview because I knew that the officer would understand and sympathise with my reasons for coming here.

In Glasgow I met a Nigerian man in a shop and he invited me to church. Everyone was an African at the church, including the pastor, and at the end of the service we were served African food prepared by the congregation. I found a community there and felt more welcome than I had ever felt since arriving. We had events and a day trip to the sea and to Stirling which made the waiting less empty and anxious.

After one month in Glasgow I was called for interview. I was interviewed for five hours by three different people. All of them were calm and persistent, but I could tell from the way they asked me questions that there was something behind it. They did not believe me and as the hours passed I began to think what I had not thought possible over the three months I had been waiting. They did not want me here. They did not like me. The result of the interview was that I was refused permission to stay.

I felt as if I was something broken and discarded, thrown away with other broken things. I could not get over the stubborn and unruffled hostility of the officers. Perhaps you knew all along it was going to turn out like this, but I did not expect it. I really thought I would be heard differently. For the next two years my application to stay was repeatedly refused, from the beginning of 2007 until the middle of 2009. I was not even allowed to attend the hearing but afterwards I was informed that my application was refused. I don't know what would have happened without the Refugee Council solicitor who took my case. Without her, I would probably have been bundled onto a plane and returned to my assassins.

In 2009, my application at last was successful, but permission to stay did not mean the end of my arriver's tale. I was not allowed to work. My allowance, which was loaded onto an electronic card, only allowed me to shop in certain shops and for certain things. In the end I took a job working illegally a few hours a week in a motor parts shop, just for pocket money. I don't know how the police found out, but they raided my flat at four in the morning, overturned everything they could overturn and took me away hurriedly as if I was a dangerous criminal. All my papers and all my property were lost during the arrest because I was not allowed to go back and was held away out of sight as if I was a poisonous snake or an infectious animal for several months. When my case eventually came to court, I was sentenced to 12 months in prison. Twelve months for daring to take a little part-time job! Now I knew I had arrived.

I was released in 2011 only to return to the limbo I was in before. I am not allowed to work. I have now been here for eight years. I have no choice but to live where I am told to live and wait for the next hearing to allow my application to be considered. Do you know what limbo means? It means the edge of hell.

The Visitor's Tale

as told by

Hubert Moore

VICTOR. I DON'T KNOW whether that was his real name. It was what I called him, and what I shall call him this evening. I don't know whether Victor came from The Gambia, as he said he did, but it's not really a visitor's job to challenge stories.

Victor was clearly a very able young man and he had been chosen to be one of his government's elite of special soldiers. These young men were trained to track down dissidents, torture them, frighten them, maybe kill them. Victor found this work so distressing, he said, that he deserted, stole a passport, left The Gambia forever, as he hoped, and headed for this country.

Soon after he arrived, he was arrested and taken to the detention centre that I was visiting at the time. My previous detainee had been moved elsewhere and it was arranged that I should visit this young man from The Gambia, Victor.

Getting into a detention centre is of course quite a business. Reasonably enough, you have to bring identification with you – passport, driving licence, utilities bill. On one occasion I had forgotten all these, but happened to have with me a copy of one of my own books of poetry. A bit sheepishly and rather assuming that poems would prove useless when required to

41

open prison-doors, I offered my book to Reception. There was a photo of me on the back of the book, which the man at the desk gazed at scornfully for several seconds. Then, wonderfully broadmindedly, he accepted the book as identification and I was allowed in.

In one detention centre I visited, there is a deep moat with a bridge over it and a massive prison-door to go through. In another, there is a succession of smaller locked doors, each one taking you a little bit further away from your free and casual life outside, towards a life of restriction and surveillance inside.

Some of these centres have a buffer zone between the building used for reception and the actual centre. This buffer zone is a sort of yard, across which you have to walk on a designated footpath to get from one building to the other. Keep to the footpath? Or cut across?

Crossing the Yard

Between Reception
and the building not quite opposite
where Detention stutters inwards
through its seven locked doors
they've painted for the benefit
of us, the undetained,
two dotted lines to keep us
on the straight and the obedient,
crossing at right angles
a sort of yard. Right angles?
At least let's go
to visit detainees
diagonally, at wrong angles.

Arriving at the room set aside for visits, what strikes me is that this is a sort of no-man's-land, a place where the detained can come through and mix with visitors on neutral ground. Detainees can have time with their partners and children. Visitors can drink hot chocolate and so can the detainees they are visiting. We can talk confidentially to each other (I think). Without this neutral ground to meet on, it's almost unthinkable what life would be like for some of the detainees.

But it's not neutral ground of course. It's detention centre ground. This is one of those arrangements – civilised in themselves – like non-bullying policies in institutions which are designed to deter, if not actually to bully – arrangements which help an essentially inhumane set-up to seem caring and respectable.

Visits Rooms, and especially their seating-arrangements, have important things to say. To visitors they say, 'Here you can talk with detainees in a thoroughly decent, reasonably comfortable, utterly orderly place.' To detainees they say, 'Here you may sit and talk as though it were your home. But this is not your home. It is purpose-furnished to house you, but not in any way to resemble a home.'

And what about seating-arrangements? Melanie Friend is very revealing about this in her excellent book, *Border Country*. At Haslar, apparently, detainees sat on red chairs and visitors on green. In at least three other detention centres, detainees sit by themselves on a single fixed seat, and visitors on the row of two or three fixed chairs opposite.

Colour Code

Your detainee will be required
to sit on a bright red chair.
A bright green non-bullying
policy operates. No offence
is intended, no sentence
pronounced. A bright red non-
freeing policy operates. You sit
on a bright green chair when you visit.

So what's it like, sitting in a detention centre and being with a detainee? Well, this oppositeness of seats, this apparent squaring up to each other, needn't matter at all. You bring with you your warmth, your interest, a readiness to acknowledge (that's really important) and an ability to listen. The main thing is you're sitting with a fellow human being. Lovely, easy-going Samuel used to tell me about his nomadic upbringing in South Africa (he was stateless, his parents never got round to registering him). Samuel had become a member of a group of travelling actors and he'd been across the world with these actors. When he was in Vietnam, he decided he would try to get refugee status in the UK, so he flew here, only to be arrested and sent to a detention centre – where (Samuel was a rarity, a real one-off amongst detainees) he loved the life: the evenings choosing which TV channel to watch in his dormitory; the company; the leisure; the visits. I used, sometimes, to ask him how his case was progressing. Had he got a good solicitor? And he would look at me with a huge smile: 'God is my solicitor,' he would say.

How to Listen

With the ears of course, where
every story enters, spirals
in and away.
Not with the nose (though many
do listen that way). The trouble is
our bony convexities can't quite
forget the thought of themselves:
our pernickety nose, our fingers
making their point, our feet in the door.
Listen with the hollows of the body:
the ears, yes, and the eyes and the mouth
and, I recommend, the undersides
of the knees. Is the listener sitting?
Well, under the knees, unseen, concave,

a cradle, that's where the wild-eyed
stories will come, then, next day,
next month, or the next, let
slip, let spout out under the table,
what was done, where, how.

What about listening to Victor, though, The Gambia's star
tracker-down of dissidents? I think that the experience of
visiting – maybe those seven locked doors work as a sort of
protection for us, the visitors – the experience of visiting
somehow makes it possible both to empathise with Victor and
to preserve one's own separate self.

We were in the brightly lit Visits Room at the removal
centre. We must have been. We were sitting opposite each
other. Victor needed to speak, to tell me his story. So we sat,
in almost total darkness, in the front seats of an unmarked
army car. We were both of us staring at a doorway at the top
of an iron staircase that connected the street with an upper
room. There was a light on over the door of this upper room,
the only lighting this deserted little back street in The Gambia
possessed.

We were in the brightly lit Visits Room at the removal
centre and Victor needed to tell me his story. We sat side-by-
side staring at the doorway at the top of the iron staircase,
Victor fingering the trigger of the gun the army had equipped
him with. And he wouldn't miss. That was what had forced
him into this situation, his expertise with a rifle.

We sat in silence, staring up. The urgency of Victor's story
was such that his words were transformed into taut wordless
experience. We were waiting in the army car outside the
offices of a local left-wing newspaper. The journalist Victor
had been told to shoot was taking his time and my visiting-
time was almost up when the door at the top of the iron
staircase opened and the journalist appeared. We were in the
brightly lit Visits Room at the removal centre.

I was going to stand bail for Victor, so he could have a

taste of a sort of freedom in the UK. His case collapsed though; his solicitor didn't turn up and the Home Office had an easy ride. Victor was taken to Colnbrook and from there back to The Gambia. It was an utterly grim ending of his time here: removal, and the near-certainty of arrest and torture on his arrival home.

Mr Tuesday, from Sierra Leone, had a very different experience. Mr Tuesday had served at least one prison sentence when he came to Dover to await removal. He had been brought up as a child-soldier in Sierra Leone and was, I think, traumatised by that experience. He was stateless, unknown to the Sierra Leone Embassy, and he waited on and on in detention, sometimes composed, sometimes crazy. Eventually, bail was requested, and we went to London feeling rather foolish and completely without hope.

Mr Tuesday's Lucky Day

It was a Thursday when the handle
of my pan flew off and left me holding
only it and not the porridge
that was boiling up inside.
Some things turn out well. The judge
heard Mr Tuesday's case that day.
Against him there was ducking, dodging, bolting,
previous convictions, heatedness,
but, since he was so minded,
the judge said, 'Mr Tuesday, it's your lucky day!'
and granted not his understanding
but a sort of freedom which rose –
well, not freedom, not waking up
on Friday morning to no fear,
no soldier-childhood howling on
and on inside his head –
up in Mr Tuesday and poured over.
He knelt for joy and wept and punched

and disappeared, went into destitution
clutching a black sack.

Visiting detainees brings great richness into your life, both sad
and happy, but it also brings you face-to-face with waiting.
Not waiting to get in for a visit, that's nothing. It's waiting
with. If people are in prison, they have a date of release to live
for; if they are in detention, they have no date to live for.
They're waiting for whenever. And you're sitting, waiting with
them.

The Believing of Trees

There's no need to finger
the wounds of the trees
to believe them.
You can trust
tell-tale scars, branch-loss,
uprootedness.
Even their stories
don't have to be true
to be true of them.
Stand in their presence.
Breathe in time with them.
Wait with them.

The Detainee's Tale

as told to

Ali Smith

THE FIRST THING THAT happens, you tell me, is that school stops.

We are meeting in a room in a London university so that you can tell me, in anodyne safe surroundings, a bit about your life so far; I say so far because you aren't old, you are maybe 30.

We meet at the front door and follow the man who's showing us to the room. We go through several doors and down then up some stairs. We go through a lot of corridors, then some more corridors, then down more stairs and along more identical corridors, then further down again and along a corridor with lagged pipes in the ceiling above our heads. We go through some swing doors, round some corners to some dead ends. We double back on ourselves. The man, who's not sure where the room is, has to keep pressing codes into doors on our way in and then on our way back out again because we've come the wrong way or taken a wrong turning.

Eventually we find the room we're being lent for the two hours. It's a room with some tables pushed together and two or three chairs in it. There's a window with a view on to bricks and the side of a building. You put your bags down, one on each side of you, and we sit down at the pushed-together tables.

You begin to speak. You speak as if picking your way over broken glass. You are graceful in the speaking. You are a small man, dainty even, and gentle. You're so small that the two quite small rucksacks you've got with you seem large beside you.

Later, when we leave this room and go back up through the maze of university corridors, you and your rucksacks keep getting caught in the swing doors because you aren't strong enough to hold them open; the door hinges are stronger than you.

Here's what you tell me. It's all in the present tense, I realise afterwards, because it is all still happening.

So: the first thing you remember knowing is that there isn't any more school. Your mother dies when you are three, you don't remember. You never see your father, so you can't remember him. You know, from being told, that your father's family fought with your mother's family; his were Hausa, hers were Christian. So you get given by your father's family to a man in the village and for a short while there's school under the great big tree, where you sit in the shade on the ground and the teacher sits on a seat and you get taught letters and reading.

Then the school has to have money so the man you've been given to takes you to the farm.

You are six years old.

There is definitely no school on the farm.

There is cocoa, there are bananas and plantain, and the harvests run from January to December. The older kids, seven or eight and upwards, drag and carry the sacks. The younger ones, like you when you arrive, do the bagging and drying. Cocoa, you explain to me, has to be dried twice. You have to climb the tree, cut the pods, break the shell with the seeds inside then pour them into the baskets, then there's the spreading them out to dry on the leaves or on the tables. The sacks of seeds are as big as you are. You drag these sacks back in the heat. The only clothes you've got are made from the sacks you drag, shorts sewn from sack. It's hot there. Not like here. You look out the window at the bricks. Not like when it's hot here either; there on the farm it's the hottest that hot can mean.

You arrive at the farm when you're six and you run away when you are 21. That's not the first time you've run away. The first time you're 15. Hunger. Beatings. Headaches. You have a headache, you have it quite often, and you have to have the right medicine or leaves for it or you hit the earth.

One day when you're 15 and the boss isn't there, you just go. You get out. There's a road. You follow it. It isn't a tarmacked road like here, you tell me. It's kind of a dirt or dust, an earth road. Anyway the boss catches you on that earth road. There are beatings for a week, and every day between the beatings you're out to work again carrying the firewood on your head, sometimes five miles, sometimes eight, and at the end of the day the boss coming in to the room with the sleeping mats in it saying how you're not making him enough money and beating you again.

There're always beatings.

A man sometimes comes to the farm, he's in the removing business, he comes to remove the stored beans. He sees the wounds on you when you are 20, 21. He says to you on the quiet, Beaten again? You need to get out of here, he says, or you'll die.

You think about the boy called Nana, who was beaten so much that he hit the ground. He didn't wake up. He didn't respond. He just lay there. You went to work, you came back, he wasn't in the house any more. Some days later you were told he was dead and that's when they started to lock you all up at night.

You put your head in your hands, here in the nondescript university room, all the years later, in London.

A very difficult time, you say. A very very difficult time.

I've been working here for a long time and I know what

I'm talking about, the man says. You've got to get out of here.

He says he is going to help you out.

I watch you remember, now, without knowing it's what you're doing, the wounds you had then. Your left hand goes to your right forearm, then to your right leg. I notice there's a scar on your forehead too, the size of a walnut shell, like someone's at some point scooped a handful-sized piece out of you.

The man tells you to go, when everyone else is busy eating, to the latrine, and when no one can see, to go through the hedges at a certain place. He tells you where the footpath is. He tells you to follow the footpath all the way.

It's eight hours to the village. It's a day when the boss and his wife aren't at the farm. You go to the latrine. You push through the hedges. You find that path. You walk till it's dark. You meet nobody. You walk till you get to a village. A woman is cooking under a shade. She sees you. She asks you where you are going. You tell her the man's name and she takes you to a house.

You sit in this house and you hope you won't be killed.

You wait there for four hours. The man comes. He says that because they're already looking for you he has to move you tonight.

You walk almost the whole night to get to a town. You are there in a room for a week. Then the man comes back and another man with him. The other man takes your photograph. We are going to take you somewhere, he says, where you are going to be safe. This is where the white people are, do you want to go there?

You are in the town where the lorry station is for a month until the man comes back with a car. He tells you not to worry. He tells you this all the way through the local villages, all the way to the proper road. You never see that brown earth road again. From now on, instead, you see a lot of lights. Then there's no lights, then lights again. Then you're standing at the counter in the airport at the man's side and there's a girl, and another boy, and the man.

Say nothing, he says. If they ask you who I am to you, say I am your uncle.

When you get to the other airport, though, it isn't London. You don't find out for quite some time. It's just a shut room that you're in, and a warehouse. Much later you get to know that it's called Luton. The shut room is all mattresses on the floor and there are six others and you in the room. There are girls in the room above, men in the room below. That night they give you all chicken and chips and tell you the work will start early so you'd better be ready.

A van comes at 4am. Someone opens the front door. The back of the van, with its door open, is right up against the front door. You and the others get in one by one. The van door closes. It's dark in the van. You get to the warehouse. You hear the warehouse door go up. The van goes in. The warehouse door comes down again.

Room, van, warehouse. Warehouse, van, room. Four in the morning. Nine at night. Packing shoes. Ladies bags. Sorting dresses. Cleaning microwaves. They give you a cloth for this. Cleaning TVs. Cleaning fridges. They give you a roll of white rubber to wrap the electric things. They give you a winter jacket, one pair of jeans and a towel. They give you two shoes. They tell you it's cost them a great deal of money to bring you here. They say you'll be working till you've paid it all back. There aren't beatings but there's shouting. There is a lot of shouting.

Room, van, warehouse. Warehouse, van, room. Five years. Most weeks all week, 18 hours a day. You sit in silence, now, with me. You hold your head in your hands.

You meet a guy, you tell me. He's the driver. He takes a liking to you. He says he can get you out of there and find you a cleaning job in London. You trust him.

You say the word trust and it is as if your whole body fills with pain. You sit silent again for a moment.

Then London. One place to the next, one place to the

next. But you go to a church. You make some friends at the church. You tell them about your life. They tell you there are things that can be done to make this better. You can write to the Home Office, they tell you, and explain to them what's happened to you, and the Home Office will help you sort this out.

You do it. You write to the Home Office.

They come. They arrest you.

They put you in prison for six months because the passport you've got is the wrong kind.

First it's prison, then detention. That takes two years. Then they release you for six months. Then they arrest you again. Back to detention, another six months. Then they release you. Any moment now they can arrest you again. They say: *We have accepted you are a victim of human trafficking.* But to go back to Ghana? You have nobody there to go to. *Indefinite leave to remain.* That means they'll arrest you again. They can, any time. *We accept you are a victim of human trafficking. But we need to reconsider the case.*

Most of all, you tell me, you want to go to school. Right now you are in a house belonging to a man from your church, and the man who has the house lets you live there. You do cleaning, do errands, you help look after the baby. It is kind of him to let you stay. There isn't any money. You sleep in the lounge when they've gone to bed. There is a chair you can sit in. You just stay at the house, that's what you do all day, except for the days you have to report. There isn't any money for any rail or bus tickets. This is sometimes a problem. Central London to East Croydon is a long walk.

You want most to go to college, you tell me in that university, in the room borrowed for two hours. But colleges need ID. The piece of ID you have, the colleges tell you, isn't enough for colleges.

You don't tell me about what detention is like until we walk back up to street level through the interminable swing-doored corridors, up staircases that lead to other corridors.

You stop in the middle of a corridor. You look at me and you say: you would ask God *not* to send your enemies to detention, where fellow human beings treat you not like human beings.

And being out of detention, and knowing they can put you back in detention? It is all like still being in detention. Detention is never not there.

You have seen things, you tell me, with your own naked eyes. The room there in detention has a window, sure. But a window without any air. The only place air comes in is the gap under the door. And the door in detention is an iron door, and when they come to lock it they bang it. They do it on purpose, to make the great noise that it makes. And there's no privacy in detention. There's no religious privacy. This is a terrible thing, you say. And there's no medication guaranteed in detention. Not even for epilepsy, your headaches. Prison is better. At least in prison there is something to do. But not at the removal centre. They call it the removal centre, you know?

You raise your eyebrows at me.

Removal, you say. When you arrive they remove you from a life. Then they remove your phone from you. They make sure it isn't the kind with cameras. They take it away for several days, and they put it 'through security'.

But still, I'm thinking to myself as you speak. It can't be that bad. It can't be as bad as prison. And surely there's a reason to take a phone away to check it. It's for security, isn't it? It doesn't sound so bad. It doesn't sound so rough, not really, and there's a window. Albeit a window that doesn't open. A window, all the same.

I am an idiot. But I'm learning. A mere hour or two with you in a university room and I'm about to find out that what I've been being taught is something world-sized.

Later this same day I will go and visit, for another couple of hours, what it is to be a detainee, in this day and age, in our country. No, not even that: what I'll go and visit is only what it's like *to visit* a detainee.

I'll take the train to the removal centre you told me about, the very place where you've been detained then detained again, then any minute now might be detained again.

It's a place so close to a runway that the sound of the planes taking off and landing is its only birdsong. There's a jolly painted sign above the visitor centre reception desk. PROPERTY CHECK-IN, it says with a big painted tick, for correct, next to it. It's the first thing I see. Is it a joke? Is it supposed to put people at ease? It's an obscene irony, and, as I'll find, maybe the most human thing in the process it takes to visit someone here. There are creatures painted, too, on the back wall of this check-in building, and some toys on the floor beneath them for visiting kids. The painted creatures are meant to be Disney jungle creatures but one looks anguished, as if in pain, and one has huge ferocious teeth.

Everywhere else there are bright information posters proclaiming in words and symbols how people of all origins, ethnicities, religions and sexual orientations will be treated equally here.

I will have to fill in two forms. I will get given a bright red wristband. VISITOR, it says on it. (Anna, my companion for the afternoon, is a regular visitor of the detainees held in the centre, and will warn me with some urgency not to lose this wristband.) I will have to empty my pockets into a locker, all the pennies and the five pence pieces, all the bits of tissue, crushed receipts, even the little balls of fluff in the linings of the pockets. I will lock the locker door on my own ID, on everything that proves I'm me, and will get given a number instead and a lanyard. Visitor Lanyard 336.

I quite often get given lanyards in my job. At literature festivals they're used as passes into all the events or the hospitality and the green rooms. I throw away several lanyards a year without thinking. This one, the one I'll be given this afternoon, will render every other lanyard I've ever been given and ever will be given from now on nothing but a frippery. The little plastic wallet it's in will be bent as if it's been twisted over and over in someone's hands, chewed by a hundred nervous people or their children – a beaten-up lanyard, a lanyard with a history.

I will have to go through a guarded door and then through an airport scanner – no, something much more downmarket, scale down your vision, more like a body scanner would have been if this was back when I was in my twenties, 30 years ago, and was ill and was claiming invalidity benefit at the DSS and part of that process of signing on had ever involved being body scanned. Before this, a man will write down my number. He will check that I'm me from a photograph that's already been taken, a minute ago, front of house, by a security camera. After it, a woman will come out of his glass-barrier office. She will make me take my boots off. She will thump them, shake them upside down. She will go through all the pockets of the coat she's made me take off with more thoroughness than I've ever had at any airport. She will find a pencil sharpener and a spare coat button in a little button envelope in my inside pocket. She will hold them both up.

Were you going to use this sharpener to sharpen a pencil and write on this envelope? she will say. No, I'll say. I didn't even know that envelope was in there.

As I say it I will feel guilty, though I'm telling nothing but the truth.

She will put the things on a table by the scanner machine.

They may or may not be there when you come out, she'll say. We take no responsibility for what's left here.

Then, after she's searched me from head to feet, the woman will unlock a door and we'll go into a waiting space and the woman will open another locked door on the other side of the room which will open into a yard with a razor-wire fence so high and encircling such a tiny yardspace that it would pass as a literal example of surreality.

Then she'll unlock another door and we'll pass into the Visitor Centre H-Block.

There will be placards everywhere. Inside the H-Block the placards will all be inspirational messages about how good the teamwork and the care are here.

Up some stairs there'll be another security check.

Altogether there are four security checks, before you can visit someone here. Then a man will unlock a door into a big square room, somehow both bright and dim, with blue carpet tiles, blue chairs. We will be shown to a seat. The form we will have signed says we have to take the seat we are shown to, and no other seat. We will do as we're told. Someone will unlock a different door behind us. The man we've come to visit will be shown through this different door.

No, not a man, something closer to a boy – a sweet tired boy, not much past adolescence. He is Vietnamese. He will find his painstaking way in English for just over an hour, telling me he is embarrassed not to be better at speaking it. I will tell him not to worry, that my Vietnamese isn't up to much. He will laugh at this. The laugh, like a clear little torchbeam, will light up the true and profound state of this young man's dejection. Anna will tell me later he spoke no English when he arrived here, and the epic nature of the story he tells me in hard-won broken phrases, of the one-and-a-half months hidden in the back of a lorry it took to get him here, will be pretty clear even though all the time I'm trying to listen to him all I'll be able to hear are the guards of this place, three or sometimes four of them, rattling their keys and their keychains incessantly up and down the length of the room, though there'll be no one here to guard but us and one other family on the cheap blue seats.

Airless, the room, and its windows barred and perspexed – and suddenly I'll understand what you were telling me this morning, about how a window, when no air can come through it, isn't the same thing as a window. You didn't even mention the bars.

I will ask the boy I'm talking to if the windows in this room are the same as the window in his room. Yes, he'll say. Do they have those bars on them? I'll say. He will nod gently. I will ask him what the food is like here. The guards, male and female alike, will walk up and down, shaking their keys. It's okay, he'll say.

He'll have his dictionary in his hand, a Pocket Vietnamese-English paperback. Its spine will be several times broken. The guards will jaunt up and down the room, joking with each other over and above our conversation and the whole time I'm there I will feel the paper edge of my VISITOR band round my wrist rough under my sleeve – I say paper, but I suppose I mean plasticised paper, because later when I try and rip it off I can't, it won't tear, and I'll have to remove it with scissors – I will feel it keenly, the whole time, the reminder that I can leave. I will long to leave.

Meanwhile the young man will be looking overjoyed at the slip of paper Anna has given him, which means he can receive a little blank notebook she's brought for him, though he won't see it for several days because it's got to go 'through security', though already we will have spent quite a long time, when we arrived in 'check-in', filling in forms about the notebook and having the notebook weighed and processed. He will say, several times, how delighted and grateful he is to have had visitors. Two visitors! Anna came! And another person! Like he can't quite believe his luck. Again this moment of brightness will mean I catch the real low ebb of his spirit.

He will tell us in broken English that his mother, at home, is ill right now, how she doesn't have a phone, and how someone from home has phoned him and told him. He will tell us he told his friend to tell her how he is fed and has a bed to sleep in. He doesn't want her to worry, he will say. He will rub his forehead with his thumb between his eyes above his nose, trying to get to the right words. He will struggle, again, for polite enough, good enough words of apology about his English not being better.

Then it's back to the H-Block reception and back through the barbed wire coiled yard. The man unlocking the doors will small-talk Anna and me about the weather. It'll be a grey, grey English day, the day I go to the detention centre. My pencil sharpener and button will still be on the table and, as we go out, Anna will tell me she is surprised I managed to get through and keep both my pairs of glasses since, a couple of weeks before, she'd been disallowed a pair of clip-on shades she sometimes wears over hers and they'd sent her back to 'check-in', made her check in all over again.

We'll go out to the carpark in the regular noise of the planes, another taking off, another one landing as we drive along the barbed wire airport fences through the new no-man's-land.

After I get home, because I'll finally have sensed the real depth of depression in the young man I've just met, I'll do a bit of digging around in what information there is, to see if there's such a thing as therapeutic help for people in detention.

There isn't.

Even if you're traumatised? Even if, when you arrive there, you've seen deaths, been tortured? It isn't provided. Even if you've got a mental illness? Like schizophrenia? Surely the place is full of people with post-traumatic stress disorder? Since nobody leaves home for no reason. Nobody crosses the world crushed in a crate in a lorry, drinking his own urine for one-and-half months; nobody gets flung on a plane from one trafficking destination to another, without terrible mental consequence.

For terrible mental consequence what there is is isolation, where the light is on 24 hours a day, where there's no sheet on the bed and nothing else in the room, and where Security check on you every 15 minutes.

When I find this out, I'll think of you and the epilepsy, and the beatings, and something you said in passing about how difficult, in detention, it is, to get the simplest medication.

Anyway, I'll be out of there, and on my own safe way home. Anna will drive me to the station. When we get there, she'll lean over, open the door for me and thank me for making the journey today.

Me? I'll say. Making a journey? Today?

I'll think of the young man in the lorry. I'll think of you

on all your roads, the road between the gone school and the farm, the first dirt road the time the boss caught you, the ground coming up to meet you when you fell with the headaches, the footpath to the village, the brown earth road you didn't see again when the road to the airport took you to another country.

I'll think of me asking you if you ever had visitors in your own time at the removal centre, and of how your face softens when I do for the only time in our talk.

Yes, you say. Mary.

Then you don't say anything else.

This morning, in the university room, just before we attempt to find our way again around that building, I ask you if you'll mind showing me the piece of paper that they give you as the proof of who you are – the proof that's not enough, when it comes to ID, for colleges.

I watch you go through your bags. I realise, by the length of time it takes you to find it, that it is a very painful thing I've asked you to do. The longer it takes the more terrible I feel for having asked you to find it and show me.

But there it is at last. You unfold it there between us. It's an A4 piece of paper, a photocopy whose ink is creased and flaking, beginning to disintegrate in the folds.

I pick it up. I hold it in my hand.

What kind of a life are we living on this earth when a photocopied piece of paper can mean and say more about your life than your life does?

On the train home this evening, I'll think of the moment you say to me, as we're saying goodbye: people don't know about what it's like to be a detainee. They think it's like what the government tells them. They don't know. You have to tell them.

On that train home, and all these weeks and months later, I'll still be thinking of the only flash of anger in the whole of your telling me a little of what's happened to you in this life so far.

It was a moment of anger only. It surfaced and disappeared in less than a breath. Except for this one moment you're calm, accepting, even forgiving – but for these six syllables, six words, that carry the weight of a planet, weight of the earth – yes, earth, like those roads there under all our feet, whatever surfaces we cover them with, under all our journeys, the roads you walked between one place and another in the mix of fear and hope and the dark falling.

But when I came to this place, when I came to your country, you say.

I sit forward. I'm listening.

You shake your head.

I thought you would help me, you say.

The Interpreter's Tale

as told to

Carol Watts

HE MAY NAT SPARE, al thogh he were his brother;
He moot as wel seye o word as another
— Geoffrey Chaucer, Prologue to *The Canterbury Tales*

Your duty is to interpret *everything* that is said.
— Home Office, *Code of Conduct for Registered Interpreters*

Here is a passage of words.
My words are given in evidence.
My words form the skin of another's arrival.
On the surface they might seem untroubled.
Like the surface of a lake.
They might seem like that to you.
As if law has a calm and liquid grammar.
Settled even in transit.
I know more about journeys than I can say.

My words follow the lines of motorways.
They know the violence of borders.
Sometimes they wait to see if they are lucky this time.
Just once is all it takes.
Sometimes they are burned off like fingerprints.
Words always grow back.

They wait.
I carry them from there to here.
Here.

I will tell you word for word.
My word for hers.
I say *I*.
I say I for her or his I.
I came from Eritrea.
I was shackled.
I saw people die in the desert.
That day I came out of the lorry I felt I had been born for a
second time.

Word for word.
I am not believed.
I am believed when she is not.
You need to understand, I tell her.
This is how it works here.
They will not believe you more if you shout louder.

Let me give you a word.
Let's say: brother.

> My brother gave me money to leave.
> My brother sent me money to leave.

Between giving and sending are continents.
Geography intervenes, a salience of stories.
Colonial maps carved up by naming and verbs.
In giving, you might understand some closeness, as if he had
come into the house that morning.
Pressed into my hand.
Take this.
Go now.

In sending, a necessary distance.
As if my brother, without rights or a bank account,
perhaps in Israel, already a migrant, had found a way to
help me leave.
Mobile contact.
A choice of two words her story relies on, in me.
Giving and sending.

Truth's kinship.
Shatters or holds us.

I say brother. That is, uncle.
So it was not her brother who helped her?
Her story isn't stacking up.
I say brother, meaning the brother of my father.

> My uncle gave me money to leave.
> My uncle sent me money to leave.

One word weighed, along with another.
Know that the *c* in your word uncle sounds like the *k* in
our maternal brother, *ako*.
An ear wants to find a meeting place in a word, to catch in
sound that switch of the heart before translation.

Listen: c c k c c c k k k
A crack in a remembered voice.
Insistence of water in the mind: like a dripping tap, when
the voice dries up.
A journey becoming voiceless.

A simple sound c: hearing hope for equivalence in families.
A simple sound c: as if we begin from the same generous
place in body and language.
A simple sound c: is her distress.
Her whole body may be ransomed by it.

I am not believed.
I am believed, but she is not.
c: credible.

That day she hurled all her naked words at the judge.

I must translate everything that is said.
Find the words closest to obscenity.
Embellish nothing.
But in the saying so much present remains unsaid, obscene.
Pressing around, like faces of the dead, or ghosted memories.
Crowds of wishes.
Fear. Absence. Oxygen. Children. Mothers. Clandestine.
Freedom. Risk.
Better life. I miss you.
Pass or die.
Words suck the air from vast containers.
Learn not to breathe so they won't tell we are all here.
Knock on arrival.

Words are spoken in relief.
Words try and move things along for now, as if later it may
come good.
I ask: 'If you know it, can you tell me?' so that stories aren't
compelled to fill in the gaps, as if politeness demands it.
Respect is a freight, it can tie words up and bind you.
I will tell you what you want to hear because of it.
I will not hold your gaze because of it.
How do you receive her?
No one is spared.

There was a road trip I took.
Years after my own journey to Europe, across five states in America.
At one point I got out of the car on a freeway.
There were seven lanes on each side.
I closed my eyes and imagined the country as it would have
been, with buffalo.

Under tarmac and concrete.
I thought: we have raped this land.

There is no freeway across these deserts.
No line on the map but tracks.
Satellites might find them, each time they orbit.
Turning earth to grid, motion to drone ways.
Noticing the scurry of beetles to escape the heat.
The helix motion of snakes, the roaming of dunes and stones.
The pickups are crammed with people, they are transferred
to larger trucks.
The convoys fly across, their drivers are often high.
Escaping armies and other gangs, kidnappings, raids.
They break down, have to be dug out.
Overturned in the speed and sand, people are buried where they fall.
So many unseen unspoken bodies, as many and more as
make it to the sea.

I heard them threaten to take her organs.
I was shot at by snipers.
I waited in the house of a man with a tank in his garden.
I was packed in cartons of washing powder.
I saw people taken from containers and hung by the side of the road.
I was detained.
I was mobile (and therefore a criminal)
I was immobile (and therefore a criminal)
I wrapped my phone in plastic.
I flew over sand and now I meet the shore.
Now a leaky boat. Now a port. Now a train. Now a lorry.
Now you.

Words are tarmac and concrete.
They can be prison houses or their unlocking.
We build cities from them around our freeways.
We walk and occupy them, they feel given to us.
How our words secure us.
We, you, us. I.

There is breeze around them, they float, they extend as far
as we choose.
How far does brother reach?
How strange is sister in her travelling?
Might one word be said as well as another?
A poem in Tigrinya: Alowuna, Alowana.
We have. We have.
Men and women.

Beneath the tarmac.
Outside the exchange of word for word.
Messages scratched on the walls of caves.
Money is a tentacular tax, weighs us all, weaves its tracks,
buys private armies, worms into border guards,
into officials, into legions of translators, phones, the ear.
Money works with the season.
The tax we all pay.

The blowback of bodies.
Cruelty without limit.

Nothing that cannot be done to them.

No punctuation to give this history reasonable measure.

The longest sentence could never span the devastation, tell
this story into available maps, translate this indifference.

As the truth it is.

Your duty is to interpret everything that is said.
Find composure.
Listen.
Speak.

Everything is at stake each time.
Everything.

The Appellant's Tale

as told to

David Herd

YOU TELL ME YOUR story on Monday March 30th 2015, in an office building by a crossing on the road out of Crawley. As you speak I take notes, asking you to pause periodically. You talk slowly and, in case I miss something, I make a recording on my phone. When you are done and the room is quiet, I ask if you wanted to tell your own tale. You said no, in the interests of security, you wished to remain anonymous.

That's how it is.

You are 63.

When you told me you were 63, I said you don't look it. [At this point in the conversation the phone records laughter.] You came to this country in 1984, to join the BBC World Service.

Margaret Thatcher's second term. Approximately half a lifetime. More than long enough to get acquainted. You tell me about events. Children. The usual sequence of addresses. We touch base at Lewisham in the early '90s.

Water under the bridge.

Which is how it goes.

We have two hours. The room is fit for purpose. Your voice is calm and carries story and as you speak I stop hearing traffic. Patiently you tell it. Step by step.

You lived in Kano State. You worked in radio and television. You have a voice, I realise, for broadcast, that we may understand what you say. Plainly. You joined the World Service for which you were interviewed in Nigeria and even in Nigeria you had to receive security clearance before you arrived in the UK.

There and then.

This was 1984.

You were given features that you translated into one of your languages: Hausa.

When you were in Kano you first heard news of where you lived from the BBC. You say this in passing, that the BBC broadcasts stories of the world to the people of the world, that people get the truth from the World Service.

That's how it is. What you are telling me is a story of empire. You mention in passing that you were at liberty to decide which stories to translate. Part of the movement is centrifugal. Sometimes you would broadcast comedy. And you tell me in villages in Nigeria, people listened on transistors.

Translation is sensitive.

In a news story, mistranslation can result in conflict.

You picked up your work permit at a British consulate in Kano, and then you came and worked for the BBC. And that work stopped the way work stops. And in Nigeria there were coups. And so you picked up a trade, this time as a plumber, and each month you paid tax and National Insurance. This is a song of occupations and so the bass note is work. And each month you worked you made a contribution until all the working made half a lifetime. Until one day, in Croydon, the state showed up and you were required to prove it.

Prove it.

There and then.

What you tell me is there and then.

You tell me that on 12th August 2012 the UK Border Agency showed up at your door. It was 6am. And what they said is they were acting on a tip-off. And you weren't dressed. And you shared the flat. And when you let them in it is you they started to question.

You.

What tip-off?

You are now the appellant.

What follows is an appellant's sequence of events.

You give them your name and your date of birth and show them evidence of National Insurance contributions and tax. And they call the Home Office and the Home Office confirms you and says you have no criminal record.

Anyway they arrest you.

You say it is because they ask you what you do. This is a song of occupations. You tell them before you were a plumber you were a journalist. When you tell them this, the senior UKBA officer jumps. There were four of them in your room, trawling through your things. He tells you that journalists are giving them headaches.

So they arrest you. There and then. Even though a person can be given a warning.

It is 6am. Something has fallen. Without warning they just grabbed you in. They take you in handcuffs to Croydon Police Station. You are wearing jeans and a t-shirt. They don't allow you to take any evidence.

It is a crucial detail. The evidence is your contribution, the song of your occupations told in National Insurance and tax, which you have kept and they don't let you take. So they close the door behind you. You don't know what that means yet. I forget to ask how heavy handcuffs weigh.

You learn afterwards that they ransacked your room. They say in 28 years you must have left the country. You say you haven't, because you haven't, only now that they have detained you, you have to prove it.

Prove it.

They say you need a solicitor, which you haven't got, and they don't take you to Croydon Police Station, they take you to Electric House. And they leave you there for 12 hours in a room with no telephone reception.

You.

The appellant.

Only you don't exactly realise yet you are the appellant; that the doors are closing; that it doesn't matter how much water is under the bridge; nor that your daughter was born in Britain; that you were invited here and are entitled to stay; that you have made your contributions; that you have been public and your situation is all in order; that for half a lifetime this is the place you have made your way.

They take you to Brook House.

It was then that you realised.

What you realised was, you were in a detention centre for illegal immigrants.

Like a hammer.

You realised it like a hammer.

I ask if you knew about detention centres before.

You said no.

I asked if you knew where Brook House was.

No.

So now you don't know what is happening and you don't know where you have come. You are taken upstairs and you can see the airport and you can see the planes. And you start asking questions and people tell you this is what they do. When they process you and you don't have a solicitor, that's it; they bring you here and then they put you on a plane.

The rhyme is flat: plane/plane. From Brook House you can see the whole runway. And in process time this is 15 hours later, except that you have been here nearly 30 years. And now you are standing, watching the charters, all the way from taxi to take off.

You.

The appellant.

They say, 'Just sign here.'

You said you weren't signing anything. You were a journalist once. You said you wanted to read it first. What it said was: you gave your consent to be deported.

Sign.

No.

You tell me the documents have a number of pages; one after the other, so if you sign one you sign them all.

Carbon copies.

If you sign it, it goes through to the next one. Confirmation for anybody who needs it that you wish to be deported.

That's the moment you resolved not to trust the UKBA. There would be other moments. A week later a man from the Home Office came. He showed you your file. 'Look,' he said, 'this is what we have about you.'

'According to our records you have been here so many years you are qualified for leave to remain. So I want to know,' said the Home Office, 'what you want to do. Because this is a detention centre for removal. You have to tell me what you want to do. You had enough? You want to leave the country? Or you want to stay?'

You tell him. So he writes: STAY.

I am taken by the meanings. Verb. To remain in the same place. To live somewhere temporarily as visitor or a guest. Except in

Scottish or South African, where it means live permanently. Also to stop, or delay, or suspend or postpone. As in, a stay of execution. As in a check on judicial proceedings. To secure or steady. As in the supporting wire or cable on an aircraft. From the Latin, to stand. From the German, be firm.

I write 'stay', as you say STAY, and this should be the end of the story. Only the ambiguities run deep and the language wants to have it both ways.

'Good,' he says, 'STAY.' And then he showed you the document. And then he says: 'Do you have any evidence of what you have been doing all these years?'

Prove it.

This is where the real becomes deeply disturbing; the administrative surreal in ways only Kafka could tell. The way a person who starts the day one thing becomes something completely other. To say it Kafka's way: the most profound metamorphosis.

You, the appellant.

You tell him you have a letter from the Inland Revenue saying you have been contributing tax and National Insurance for over 25 years. He says, 'Where's this letter?'

You say, 'It's in my house.'

He says, 'You need to bring this letter to us.'

You say, 'If you'll let me go there with a police escort, I can bring it back.'

Only this man is from the Home Office and the people holding you are UKBA. And in their opinion you must have travelled and since you can't prove otherwise you have to be detained.

The contortion runs deep. Chaucer would have known what to do with it. One of those impossibly twisted double plots. Only the contortion is a knot. And you are the person held within it. And all the while outside time is passing and your landlord takes the decision you are not coming back.

So he bags up your things, everything including the letters, since he has a room to let and this is a familiar tale. And he puts all the documents in a black bag and he puts the black bag outside for collection. Which is where we leave it. Only at this moment you don't know it is there. And you can't be released until such time as you have it.

Caught.

And so it goes.

On.

Indefinitely.

While you were in Brook House three men attempted suicide.

You never saw that before.

In Brook House you saw it three times.

People who have never been in detention, they think if you are in detention you must have committed a crime. People start running. Before long you are dead completely.

One morning they came again. Again at 6am. For the sake of argument, let's call it their operational method. They just open your door and they tell you you are leaving. They tell you you are going to a removal cell.

They take you to a detention centre near Heathrow.

You remember the name: Colnbrook.

Brook meaning stream.

Brook meaning, tolerate, allow.

They tell you people from the embassy are coming and they will confirm who you are. And once your identity is established then you will be deported.

Except that you know the women. We wonder about the chances. They tell you the Border Agency have asked them for a travel document but you say no, you have a case, because you are applying for bail and since they know you they believe you and so they refuse the UKBA. They say they cannot issue removal documents because you have a case outstanding.

Pending.

They send you back.

This is the song of the appellant.

And because it is the song of the appellant is it also a history of bail, that ancient privilege known to Chaucer so that his pilgrims might walk safe; whereby many of the king's subjects hereafter may be long detained, in such cases to their great charge and vexation.

To their great vexation.

This is the appellant's story.

You appear before the bail tribunal via video-link. You are visibly detained. The UKBA speak to the judge directly. They tell the judge they have issued removal directions against you.

They haven't. That was a lie.

You witness numerous lies.

It matters you are not in the courtroom. The judge accepts what the UKBA says.

He tells you, you are going to be removed because nobody knows who you are. You have been in detention eight weeks and you haven't provided evidence.

You, the appellant.

Nobody has actually charged you with anything.

Pending deportation, you are refused bail.

This is a song of mistrust and now you know you can't believe anyone.

Sometimes – you say politely – mental issues arise.

Once more they come at 6am. This is not something you get used to: security officers banging at your metal door.

This time they take you to Portsmouth.

You pause to reflect. Make no mistake, you tell me: these movements are deliberate.

Because now you have lost your solicitor, because he can't visit you from London. This is the logic. And now you are in a prison and all the restrictions are worse. You can't use your phone, except when your door is unlocked, and then you have to walk to the end of the garden for a signal. And it is almost impossible to call a representative because it is only in this window that you can use your phone.

Everything is deliberate.

'You know what they did?'

You say it patiently, like even now, you wish you didn't have to believe it. In that moment of being traumatised, not knowing where you are or what you are doing, with no solicitor and no window when you can realistically call, they faxed you forms to apply for leave to remain that you must complete because they give you a deadline. Except the forms they send are the kind of forms you can only use if you are applying from abroad.

Everything.

Deliberate.

What they want to prove is that you have left the country.

Now you have signed a form that tells the court you have left, that places you somewhere else.

Your next solicitor will ask why you signed. You tell him you couldn't call. Everything is happening all at once. He tells you this is a big mess.

Sign.

You sign.

'I had to do this.'

Temporarily the transformation is complete. You pause as it dawns again: the magnitude of the situation.

You, the appellant, have signed your status away.

Pause.

Pause.

There are no accidents.

And all the degradations you are describing are taking place in real time.

Indefinitely. No sign of resolution. Outwith the evidence outside a house in Croydon. In a plastic bag which even now you don't know exists.

Kafka not Chaucer.

You are returned to Gatwick. And you are faxing for a new solicitor. Faxing, faxing because you have no credit on your phone. Which is what it comes down to. No credit. Not till Gatwick Detainees Welfare Group find you. And when you apply again for bail the UKBA requests anonymity.

I ask what anonymity means.

You say the way it looks, you are a nobody. It means you have no story. If you are given anonymity the UKBA can say you have not stayed here for so long. And nobody could establish whether you have been here, where are your friends, where are your connections. You are anonymous. Nobody knows you. That's what you thought it was.

Form IAFT2: 'Anonymity, when granted, will result in the tribunal removing your name from all published documents.'

No story, you tell me.

The Judge refuses the UKBA. They tell him they have issued removal directions against you.

That was a lie. They hadn't. The judge believed them.

Think about it, you say, you could be in detention forever.

Months.

Years.

And all the time this process.

Mistrust is part of the process. What you depart from is not the way. Until finally it is plain you cannot be deported. So after six months you receive a letter granting temporary admission.

Not bail, I ask.

No. Temporary admission. And therefore no assistance. Only an instruction to go to your surety's address. Only they hadn't checked and your surety has four children and his house is small and it just is not possible for you to stay.

So the woman at Brook House calls your caseworker and you could hear she was angry. And you recall it was January and in the sky there was snow. And now the woman was in tears because your caseworker told her you should just be taken out and left in Croydon. And if you didn't go to your surety's house they would pick you up again.

Like a circle.

And she said no, he is not going anywhere. He is an old man.

I will not be a party to that. Eventually they relent and two weeks later they tell you to go to your old address.

6 St Martins Hill, Thornton Heath.

You remember the date.

January 10th, 2013.

Dates matter. You came here in 1984. You worked for 28 years and all the while you were working you paid National Insurance and tax. This is a song of occupations. First you were a journalist and then you were a plumber. Until one morning, in Croydon, the state showed up.

And then you were released. And all that time nobody had charged you with anything and the people detaining you had repeatedly told lies to the court. And the day it happened you headed home, and you rang the landlord to tell him and he was sympathetic but he told you you don't have a place anymore.

'All your things are gone. We threw them away because they thought you'd never come back. The only stuff you have left is rubbish. I don't know if the bag is still there.'

'David, I went to the garden; I opened the bags; and I found all those documents of National Insurance and tax. The first day I arrived I saw it. The second day I went to my solicitor and the solicitor was shocked in absolute disbelief, because they had written letters to the Inland Revenue for months and they had refused to comply. "This is a miracle," my solicitor said. "Where did you find them?"'

And so you told him, you said it was in the garden. You have lost your TV, your clothes, your everything, gone. But these letters were in bags in the garden.

Nobody present had thought to throw them away.

Which should be the end of the story, only this is the song of the appellant. The terms of your temporary admission are: you can't work and you have to sleep at your Landlord's address. So every day is a negotiation and though you had the letters now and you could prove it, yours is an appellant's story and everything is in suspense.

Pending.

Outwith.

You tell me you were begging, desperate.

Until Lauren from the Welfare Group said you should contact your MP. Your MP wrote to the Home Office and after he wrote, the Home Office replied within five days: 'Dear Mr North, We apologise for the delay.'

Silence.

You let that hang.

The recording is running.

I ask when finally you got leave to remain.

16th July 2014.

5 days before your 63rd birthday.

11 months after you were first detained.

You say that thoughts come back.

You used to wake up at 6am, panicking and sweating because

they came for you three times. Banging on the door. Sometimes they put you in a room of two. And then in the morning you wake up to find your roommate has been deported.

Think about it.

One day the bus actually came. There were 13 of you. You were the last and they were checking everybody in. Right, they asked, how do you feel now you are going to be deported. That was when you were passing. Then the Home Office stepped in. That one is not going anywhere.

You collapsed. It was too much. You saw this massive bus and everybody ahead of you was being checked in. You don't know if they knew you weren't going anywhere. Anyway they put you through that hell.

You pause.

The traffic is quiet.

I ask if there is anything you would like to add.

'No,' you say, calm.

'That's my story.'

The Dependant's Tale

as told to

Marina Lewycka

THE NIGHTMARE ALWAYS STARTS in the same way: a big man standing at the foot of my bed, shouting at me. 'Get up! Hurry hurry hurry! Pack up your stuff! We've come to take you away.' I call out to my parents, but they've disappeared. My little brother starts yelling, but the man just shouts again. Sometimes it's a nightmare, and sometimes it's for real.

The first time it ever happened, it was for real, but it felt like a nightmare. I was only eight, and my brother was seven. We were fast asleep in bed in our house in Bradford, when suddenly the light was switched on and the big man in a uniform was standing there. In fact there were four men in the room, all wearing the same dark uniforms. I tried to scream, but it just came out as a squeak.

'Where are you taking us?'

'We're taking you home.'

'But this is my home!'

'Don't argue. Just get your clothes on, and pack what you need.'

'Where are my mum and dad?'

'They're downstairs. No, you can't talk to them. Just pack up all you need to take for your whole family.'

I was only eight, so I had no idea what to take. I took my favourite toys, and some bed-sheets and towels that were in the room, but I didn't think of taking clothes or anything useful. My brother was screaming. I asked to go to the toilet, and I had to leave the door open, so they could watch me. That was horrible. When we'd finished packing, we were taken downstairs where our parents were being watched by four other officers – two per person, so there were eight altogether in our little house that morning. My mother was crying, but I couldn't comfort her.

We still weren't allowed to talk to our parents, but then we were all quickly bundled outside into a van. It was still dark outside. The van had a wire cage in it, and we were locked in the cage as though we were wild animals or something. It felt terrible.

'We're taking you home,' they kept saying, as we drove away and left our home behind.

Later I found out that they weren't policemen or soldiers at all, they were called 'escorts' and they worked for a private company that is contracted to the government. I don't know who draws up the guidelines for how they should treat people they are deporting, or keeps a check on how they behave. It seems a bit incredible that they thought they needed four grown men to manage me and my seven-year-old brother – we were so dangerous!

Hours later, we arrived at a place called Yarl's Wood. We were given a bag to take in what we needed, and my parents got upset that we had packed so much useless stuff. But of course we didn't know what to take. My first impression of Yarl's Wood was a funny smell, like a hospital and long grey-painted corridors with lots of doors that had to be unlocked and locked each time you went through. We were given two adjoining rooms, my parents in one, my brother and me in the other, all the furniture was bolted to the floor and there were bars on the windows – but one of the worst things was they could just come into your room at any time. We had no privacy. If I stood on tiptoe and held onto the bars I could see a small playground down below enclosed by high walls. That was the only place we could be allowed to feel like children.

We stayed 24 days in Yarl's Wood. Each day started with a roll-call at 6am when they marched into our rooms and counted us: one, two, three, four. Breakfast was from 7:30 to 8am, it was always the same: eggs, toast, cornflakes, in a big canteen and everybody sat with their families. That sounds quite nice, doesn't it? But it was actually quite scary, because there was often someone who was screaming, or panicking, or having a tantrum, and banging and shouting. Once we overslept and missed breakfast, and that meant we would not have anything to eat until lunch at one o'clock. Then my dad lost it and started shouting and crying. It was terrible to see him like that. My parents were quite good at hiding it, but suddenly at times like that you realised the stress they were under.

At that time, I didn't know anything about their application for refugee status and why they kept on getting turned down – I just knew what it felt like to be eight years old and not know where we were going or why my parents were so upset, or when the big man out of my nightmares would appear again at the foot of my bed. Later on, I learned that my parents couldn't stay in the former Soviet country where they came from, because my mum is a Christian and my dad is a Muslim, and mixed marriages are not allowed and people said they would kill us. When my brother and I went to school, some kids would always pick a fight with us, because our parents were different.

Everybody in Yarl's Wood was in the same situation or worse, they did not know whether they would be allowed to stay or what would happen to them if they were sent home. Some people went a bit crazy, and my mum got sick with asthma and high blood pressure and panic attacks; she got very thin and nervy and she didn't seem like my mum at all. Whenever she went to the medical centre, they said, 'Are you sure you're not just making it up? Go and take a paracetamol.'

It was me that had to look after her, and I had to be like a grown up even though I was only eight.

During the day, we spent our time in the library or the playground, or sometimes we went to school. It wasn't a proper school, we didn't learn anything, we just did things like colouring-in to pass the time, but one of the teachers was nice and encouraged us. Most of the security guards just shouted at us like we were just animals.

One day in the dining room I met a young Kurdish girl, and we made friends. She was so funny and lively, she wasn't scared of anything, and that made me feel better, and after that we stuck together.

After about three weeks, we suddenly got news that Mum and my brother and I could be released. It felt good to be free, and I was so glad to say goodbye to Yarl's Wood. Little did I know that I would see that horrible place again. We were taken back to our house in Bradford, but our dad was not allowed to come – they took him to a place near Oxford. Being at home without him was scary, because we never knew when we'd see him again. Mum was crying all the time, and she got very dependent on me, even though I was classed as the dependant.

Then after about three months, it happened all over again – the banging on the door at 6am. The big man at the foot of my bed shouting, 'Quick, hurry, get up and pack! We've come to take you home!'

This time they took us straight to the airport, where we met up with our dad. The guards were shouting at us, saying, 'If you try anything, we'll have to handcuff you.' So we didn't struggle, we just got on the plane, and I don't know what happened next, because I fell asleep, and when I woke up we were in our country.

It felt so strange being there – although they said we were going home, it was not like being home at all but somewhere strange and unfamiliar. When we got back, Mum blacked out and was rushed to hospital, and we were separated from our dad; we had nowhere to go so we just kept on moving around to different people's houses.

Then Mum tried to come back to England again. I was so happy to be back in Folkestone again, because I felt safe. This time we were not sent to Bradford, we were sent to Wales. Mum started to cry at first because it was unfamiliar, but it was very nice. I went to school and started to make friends. Everything seemed normal, but Mum kept saying, Don't buy anything new, clothes or toys, don't get too settled, because we may have to move soon!

But that wasn't the end of the nightmares. They carried on, always a bit different, but always the same. One night I had a dream that I was lying on a sofa in the dark when a man walked in and started shouting to get up and hurry, they were taking us home. I woke up screaming, then I realised that it was just a dream, and I fell asleep again. Then it happened again, and this time it was real. It was the same thing over again. This time there were six people all in the bedroom, including a woman who was taking photos of us, and Mum was once more on her own downstairs while we packed.

They got us into the caged van – but this time we only went as far as the police station. Mum told them we hadn't had a reply to our letter – our case was still pending – and they made us wait inside the van while they checked, so we were taken back home.

That time of waiting was the worst, or maybe it was because I was older and could remember more. I started to be scared of everything; I had the nightmare early every night. My brother started wetting his bed. Mum was anxious and got very thin. She kept the door locked all the time, and wedged it with a rolling pin.

Then a couple of months later, it happened all over again – the banging on the door in the early morning, the shouting, the packing, the caged van. Only this time, one thing was different. I had a friend at school, and I managed to ring her, and she told her parents, and lots of people came from all over the area and gathered outside our house, protesting and pleading with them to let us stay. It felt much better, because we were no longer alone, but people could see what we were going through. It didn't make any difference, we still had to go. They took us all the way back to Yarl's Wood. They wouldn't even let us get out to go to the toilet, and Mum was so embarrassed because she weed in the van.

Once again we were in Yarl's Wood. To my delight my old friend was there too. She said it was the fourth time they were trying to deport her. But this time it was different. Far more people were now aware of the situation in Yarl's Wood, through the Yarl's Wood Befrienders and there was a big campaign building up with people including Natasha Walter and Juliet Stephenson, for women and children not to be held there. Through them we were also put in touch with a solicitor, who had more experience of immigration law, and wasn't just trying to take our money and do nothing. I found out later that there had been a big campaign for us in Wales, too.

In spite of all that, though, we were still told to prepare ourselves for deportation. We got all packed up and I said goodbye to my friend. This time, I told my mum, I wasn't just going to go quietly, I was determined to protest. At 2:30 in the morning they came and took us out to the airfield. I was praying that the flight would be cancelled, or that we would get a letter at the last minute. Then just as they opened the door of the van, the guard's phone rang. Everything went quiet. 'Yes,' I heard him say. 'Yes.'

Our deportation had been cancelled. Our new solicitor had succeeded in stopping it at the last minute. Mum fainted. I just sat in the van holding my breath until the plane took off without us.

We were taken back to Yarl's Wood, and everything seemed as before for a couple of weeks. Then one day we were called by the teacher to go to reception. I was terrified because I was sure it would be something bad. But we were told we would be going back to our old home in Wales.

It was lovely being back in our old house, and seeing my friends, and all the people who had been campaigning for us and signing petitions for us while we were away. While we were in Wales, we also got news from our dad. He was in France, and he had been given refugee status there, and he would apply for residence to come to the UK. In 2009 we were all reunited. Now I'm a student in my third year at LSE, reading law.

So you might think this is a story with a happy ending, and in a way it is. But in a way, I feel I was robbed of my childhood, I was forced to grow up and have to deal with things no child should have to deal with. Whatever people think about the rights and wrongs of immigration, it can never be right to treat children like this. From time to time I still wake up in the night shaking with fear when I hear a loud banging or shouting. But then I realise it's only a nightmare.

The Friend's Tale

as told to

Jade Amoli-Jackson

I SPOKE TO A very good lady, Anj Handa of the People Help People Foundation, on the 20th January 2015 and thought: *I have met a friend indeed.* She was great to talk to and I felt as though we had known each other for a long time.

I wanted to learn more about a client of hers whom she called 'A' but I will now call her 'Alice'. Anj first met Alice on 16th January 2014. She had found out about Alice through a friend in the Migrant Access Partnership in Leeds, who knew about her campaign to end Female Genital Mutilation (FGM). At the time of the introduction, Anj thought that Alice just needed friendship and moral support. However, on the day of their meeting, Alice confided in her that she had a Home Office return visit coming up in two days and she wanted Anj to be there with her and her daughters as she was scared.

Alice is an amazing woman in her 30s and pretty too. She has a degree in HR Management. She came to this country, pregnant with her second child, to escape the FGM of her daughters. Alice underwent FGM as a baby and has suffered physical and psychological problems as a result, especially during childbirth. How can someone be cut and stitched in this way?

Given her awful experiences, you could call Alice a victim but she refused to be one. She enrolled her eldest daughter in pre-school, she helped fundraise for the school and worked as a volunteer, helping other women in a similar position to herself. She attended church regularly and maybe her faith, along with her huge love for her daughters and friends, helped to keep her going. She booked herself onto every possible seminar on women's issues, so that she could learn more and help others in need.

Anj told me that Alice was smart and they quickly became friends even though they had completely different backgrounds. They are both women in their 30s with a lot of life experiences who just want to help other women and protect young girls. Their shared interests gave them a strong bond. I join them in that. I feel as though I have known both of them all my life, even though I have not met them in person. I have spoken to Anj on Skype and have fallen in love with her strength and what she does to help other vulnerable women.

Anj told me that on the day they met, Alice had legal representation, but she still asked Anj to be with her during the Home Office return visit. Anj said that she would if the solicitor agreed. She emailed him to tell him of her involvement and to offer her support in compiling evidence but was shocked the next day when he called Alice to tell her that he was not going to represent her through Legal Aid after all. He didn't bother to reply to Anj's email which made her angry. This was a massive blow to Alice as she had no one to represent her and Anj had to work frantically all Wednesday evening, emailing and tweeting to try to secure alternative legal help for Alice. Fortunately, Felicity Gerry QC tweeted back immediately saying that she was willing to help and that, by coincidence, she would be in Leeds that Friday. Felicity lives in Australia and had not been to Leeds for many years, so it was unexpected. Anj felt Guardian Angels were watching over them.

On Thursday, Anj attended the Home Office return visit at Alice's home. She had advised Alice that morning to take her elder daughter, whom she called 'B' but I call Bobby, to school so that she did not have to witness the meeting. It was good advice because Alice fainted during the meeting and Anj had to take her youngest daughter, R (I call her Rachel), upstairs because she did not want the little girl to witness her mum in such distress. These kinds of things can last a lifetime. The Home Office staff present were considerate and checked on Anj and little Rachel while Alice was being treated by paramedics. However, having two Home Office staff wearing full protective gear was very intimidating, even if they were gentle. While all this was going on, Rachel fell asleep in Anj's arms and slept like a baby.

It's hard not to become emotionally attached when children are involved. 'Thinking of her little smile motivates me when I'm working all hours on this case,' Anj told me later. Every time she said goodbye, Rachel would burst into tears. Anj's favourite memory of little Rachel was sitting in the back seat of her car, singing 'Hallelujah'. She thought it impressive for a toddler, who was not yet two, even if she did make up some of the words. It is a memory Anj will never forget.

On Friday, Anj met with Felicity who had agreed to help with the case through a Direct Access agreement. She went with Anj to Alice's house to meet her and sign the paperwork. She also agreed to guide Anj through the process of compiling evidence, which was a massive task to tackle in such a short time. She told me that she worked late that Friday, putting together as much information as she could within that short period. She had no idea how she would be able to fit it all in. Anj was also in the process of setting up a new organisation that aims to put an end to FGM and gender-based violence through promotion of empowerment, health and education initiatives for girls and women. Anj praised her three business partners for their support and for taking up most of the workload so that she could focus on helping Alice and her children in their time of need.

Anj felt that losing the first solicitor had been a blessing in disguise because the next day, a Saturday, Ben Davison from

Ison Harrison Solicitors, gave her a call to talk through the case. Ben agreed to put together the bundle of evidence and to represent Alice, even if he was not able to secure funding through Legal Aid.

While all these legal battles were going on, they received support from organisations such as the Red Cross. There is not much in the way of protection available in Alice's Home country, Nigeria. The main thing for Anj to do was to keep Alice and her children's spirits up throughout the waiting process. Alice suffered from depression and had to increase her medication in order to cope with the stress. Anj took Alice and the children out for walks in the park and danced around the living room with the girls but did not feel as though she was helping much. Women like Alice are separated from friends and family and have no choice about where they end up.

The day came when the work was complete and Alice asked Anj to accompany her when she took in the bundle. Anj witnessed how people had to present their cases, very personal details, through glass partitions, in a public waiting area which felt very degrading. It brought back to her the negative assumption that all asylum claimants are deemed to be liars, unless they can prove otherwise.

Unfortunately, this was also the case with Alice and the Home Office gave a negative decision on the fresh evidence that she had submitted. It appeared that they had not considered its context. In particular: the recent case law, upon which this fresh evidence was based, or the situation in Nigeria (regarding the protection of a single mother with two young children) which was clearly different from that of two years ago when her evidence was first presented.

Alice was told her case had no merit, that she would have to return to Nigeria and that she would only be able to appeal this decision from outside the UK. There might be the opportunity to challenge the decision because they had not commented on the fresh evidence, but Alice did not have

Legal Aid. Even though Felicity Gerry had offered to support Alice's case, she lives outside the UK, so that wasn't an option because Counsel may be needed at short notice.

Anj felt that Alice had been let down on a number of levels: first, by her family who subjected her and her eldest daughter to FGM (Alice had fled to the UK whilst pregnant with her second child, a girl); then by well-meaning but incorrect advice from some support organisations; third, by the solicitor who took on her claim, but then dropped her before undertaking any work; fourth, by the male judge who was utterly unsympathetic and questioned her credibility; and finally by the Home Office, who responded too hastily to the fresh evidence without considering its context, and for mistakenly publishing Alice's confidential information on their website without her permission and without offering legal recourse until later.

Alice and her children were deported back to Nigeria.

During their first ever meeting, Alice told Anj that she needed to protect her daughters. She wanted them to be proud of her when they were old enough to understand, because nobody had protected her.

The Deportee's Tale

as told to

Avaes Mohammad

IT WAS 3 O'CLOCK, he said.

A.M.

He would have known.

Sleepless heads bob perfectly with each strike of the second-hand.
In dark stagnant air, each nod a sigh and each sigh a sign of not yet.
Until it is.

Until fortress doors are commanded open, setting forth
charging boots, searing screams, bruising curses and the only
stirring felt in that cell for hours.

'Verily with every difficulty comes ease.'

And a cool draught momentarily licks away beads of settled
sweat as he's pulled and slammed face down again.

With no regard whatsoever for the rhythm of that second hand.

Cold, crushing handcuffs pierce straight to the bone, officially.

'Shut the fuck up, motherfucker. Shut your fuckin' mouth
now.' Officially.

All he asked was why they had to send him to Greece.

Like lifeless chattel devoid of any form at all, he's thrown onto
the floor below, hauled from there and torn out of this space
he'd known.

He'd cried through this. Or so I'm told.

Dared to state he didn't need this, didn't want to go to Greece.

But would rather just have someone help.

The officials, officially, never heard anything.

Showed no official interest.

Or any other kind and led him away with no regard whatsoever for the rhythm of that second hand, which simply just carried on.

Handcuffed in the car to Heathrow.

Pleads and begs and cries, all quickly quenched.

You haven't any right to say anything.

Your need to speak is not your right.

Your silence now is not your right.

Your questions, fears, this panicked will to clear yourself

Is not your right.

Airports are just a vast attempt to manage a plague of the world's travellers, foreigners, passengers and all otherers from somewhere else.

Anyone basically, who dared to move.

It's fine if you do it to ski.

Less so if you do it to live.

Perhaps it's to avoid confusing ourselves, to avoid shattering every mass-consumed illusion, which allows us to do what we do like pre-programmed post-humans belligerently aware that, should the processes of human thought and thinking be re-awakened, none of this would make sense. None of us would make sense.

And so, hiding themselves in the crevices, they lead the detained onto shadowed, secret routes, handcuffed, so all can know he hasn't earned the right to go where his feet lead. To follow the vision his sight affords.

Unlike, of course, the skiers, the fleers, the cheap holidayers,

The backpackers, gap-trackers, experience-receivers,

The lunches in suits, who discern over croutes,

How nations are bled, to give life to the fewest.

As earth ejects everyone equally and like air-bound gypsies the plane soars on, the handcuffs are taken off and his hands released.

I can see the logic. If his crime is stealing earth to stand upon, then there's no cause for concern up here.

It's strange to think what he was fighting to stay in was

nothing more than a prison cell,
A centre for the detained punishing those with no homes.
Lacerated feet so they dare not stand again,
Exacerbated breath so they daren't inhale again
Or so you'd think.
Had his breadth continued in time with the second hand
Then 8am
Like every other 8am
His door would have opened, letting in the only trace of air
Some breeze
Some movement that isn't a heart bashing its head against its chest
Until 8:45 when breakfast would have been served
Though 8:45 is probably when his eyes would have stirred,
cooled as they were by the relief of morning
Dawning at the call of an officer
Besides there's only so many eggs a boy can eat everyday.
At 8:45 he would have walked the yard
Talking to people just enough to feel their presence
Avoiding them just enough to escape their pressures
The same thought echoes: how and when they are going to leave
Watch Hashim tell the guy with no shoes how he read you
can bail yourself out with just one pound.
At 11am he'd go back to his room one whole hour before lockup.
The undiscerning eye would probably miss the independence
ringing through this.
Until 1 you bide your time,
1:30 you lunch.
At 2 everyone is out again.
Stick to the people you know.
Of those, stick to the people who know.
Of those, stick to the people who haven't yet lost their minds
'What do you mean there's no money on it. We have our
rights you know! We have to have our rights! I need a
statement, a full print-out statement. Are you listening? You all
think we are a piece of shit, don't you? Don't you?! All of you
think we are a piece of shit! Because we are not from here,

huh? Because we're not from Britain? Because we are foreigners! Well you're not! You're not gonna put my life at risk economically or politically. Do you understand? You're not! My life is an achievement and you're not going to turn me into a criminal! I've been obeying laws here for 17 years!' That's Hashim. There's no one who walks with him anymore. At 7pm dinner.

8 shower.

8:45 the doors slam shut on them again. And each one pretends to be asleep, while each one looks through one eye, regulating breath with the second hand as though trying to learn how it's done again

And yet this seemed worth fighting for.

Maybe because he just wanted to stay still.

Maybe because he wanted to breathe a little, get used to breathing a little.

Find his own rhythm.

Perhaps find his old rhythm again.

A local man

A caring kind colossal man

With colossal hands and eyes and mouth and size

Called Jim

Would heave through those fortified gates with heaps of clothes and smiles

Someone who dared to sit and look at him for longer than most looks had been.

Spoke to ask not where he's from, why he's here, but how he is, who he is?

Jim was the first.

The first one to show this young boy that he cared

Assure him that there's someone there

Encourage him, empower him, fight for this young man – that was Jim

This young child of 14 years who'd walked from Afghanistan, entering into Pakistan, lorry smuggled him into Iran

Climbed mountains, deserts, cities and the first man in

months, over half this earth, the first who asked him how he was, was this man named Jim.

That's probably why he fights to stay somewhere, to be someone colossal enough to show he cared

The sign for seatbelt lit

His wrists half-crippled, half-formed, half-human as handcuffs clicked

His first point of entry into the EU, Greece is where he would be returned to.

Apparently.

It's nothing more than that game where pinballs slowly go, only to be struck again somewhere, anywhere, away.

The Greek Police were waiting at the airport

Ready

The British Police less handed him over, more dumped him

It had all been done before, well-trodden rites

Taken by the new uniform hosts into a quiet corner, they beat him.

Why? He asked

Why do you beat me?

No place for questions this. They just did. They just did.

From the airport, a small prison where no one speaks. No officer, no official, no one to help, no one to guide and tell you.

He tried to call Jim but couldn't get through

And then a letter

Greece issues him one month, to have to leave

And so it all begins again

Hoping this time might be more successful, he sleeps in parks and finds a job picking olives preparing for yet another exodus. Another odyssey relived.

Hiding at the harbour, with all the other refugees where every hour lorries are sought to be climbed under.

Like human swarms pushing and jostling each one desperate in their quest to keep moving. In the shadows. Amidst the crevices. Just desperate to keep on moving.

If you have money you can skip the queue. Enterprise, like a

weed, takes root in every stinking pit. This is Europe after all.
Otherwise mind the police and the dogs who beat you for entering
And beat you for leaving.
Arms and legs left broken like a game children play – plucking wings off fleas then daring them to fly again.
Finding a lorry he held on.
No seats on the undercarriage
Like the rest of his tale, it's not really designed for humans.
And so he just held on.
From Greece to Italy.
A full 12 hours.
This 14-year-old.
Held on.
With all his strength.
Herculean
With all his power, to simply keep moving, to simply not be seen.
But even Hercules would fail and so did he momentarily as his leg scraped across the surface of an earth that didn't want him.
Arriving in a village in Italy he sought out Rome
Not for the beauty or the art but simply because there'd be other refugees who'd look like him
Whose darker hues could shade him.
For just enough time for his legs to be able to hold him again
This time the promised land was Scandinavia, its clean streets, kind people had been whispered about like myth.
You'll never know if you don't go.
Italy, France, Holland, Germany.
Hiding under seats in trains
Sleeping under bushes in parks
Staying well within the shadows
The shadow stretched over half a continent
Not until Germany did the first crack of light expose him,
Unveil him
To the sight of yet another uniformed official from officialdom.
Handcuffed. Again.

In court the next day he understood nothing, except that he was driven to prison.

14 years of age attempting to find a way of being in a prison made for men.

What's he doing here?

What you doing here?

Don't you speak the language?

He doesn't speak the language!

How old is he?

Too young is how old!

Oi! You too young!

Too young to be here!

With us!

Far too young!

Too young!

This is a prison! For men! What you doing here!

He needs a lawyer!

Do you have a lawyer?

This isn't human rights!

It took prisoners to claim his human rights. His being human.

It took prisoners to do that.

It took prisoners to rally around and find him a lawyer.

It took prisoners to pay his fees so a letter could be written.

Another court, another judge.

The same stock solution grasped at blindly, because no one dare take off their blindfolds.

Send him to Greece.

Another 3am came.

Another fight

Another pleading

This time by the police. To a pilot who refused to play the games of officialdom.

Perhaps with his view of the earth he'd recognized the illusion of borders.

~~The next time he was ripped out of his cell and taken to court~~

he didn't even know he was made free

Until his lawyers started to cry
And boarded him onto a train for a refugee camp in Braunschweig
From where he was told to move onto Oldenberg.
He doesn't know why.
It wasn't for him to ask questions, he just did.
If he's being allowed to live, he just will.
There was a church in that camp and a woman who'd clean it everyday.
This is a tale of where humanity hides.
In prisoners' wails, in a lawyer's tear, in a pilot's view of the world
In a woman's view of God in a child
Who took him in, embraced and gave him new life
Someone to take care of him and fight for his rights.
Someone to finally show that while we're content to send them to death
There are some amongst us who harbour life.

The Lawyer's Tale

as told to

Stephen Collis

CHAUCER'S 'THE MAN OF LAW'S Tale' is a narrative of sea migrations, of exile and refuge and exile yet again. Sea journeys are signs of rejection, betrayal, treachery, homelessness. Constance, our heroine, is driven by forces she has little control over – across the Mediterranean, out into the Atlantic – and back again. Systems of state and patriarchal power enclose then reject her; her freedom is fleeting, false – a ship in which *They han hir set, and bidde hir lerne saille*, or in which she arrives at a *straunge nacioun*, where she may yet again be *bounde under subjeccioun*.

> Giorgio Agamben: 'It is almost as if, starting from a certain point, every decisive political event were double-sided: the spaces, the liberties, and the rights won by individuals in their conflicts with central powers always simultaneously prepares a tacit but increasing inscription of individuals' lives within the state order, thus offering a new and more dreadful foundation for the very sovereign power from which they wanted to liberate themselves.'

Chaucer's Man of Law tells us precious little about the law, or himself. The 'General Prologue' only notes his desire for property: *Al was fee symple to hym*. It is not clear what

STEPHEN COLLIS

Constance's story means to him, either personally or
professionally. 'The Man of Law' remains *terra nullius*, a
spurious empty zone to claim, desire stretching its hands out
towards the unclaimed lands of claimants from their own lands
torn.

> The lawyer
> looking out to see
> croons April in
> cruellest soliloquy
> *ship that fleteth*
> *in the Grete see*
> – to make submissiouns
>   in courts *of peine and wo*
>
> knowing the truth
> one does not always
> remain intact
>   nor does the truth
> always remain intact
> and the borders
>   are no longer
>   at the border
>
> but move as magnets
> amongst iron filing statutes

Because of a complicated relation to borders, we
are trying to figure the boundaries of our present
age. I don't particularly like the term 'Anthropocene'
– isn't the *anthros* what we are trying to navigate
away from? Call it 'geophysical capitalism': the era
in which our economic activities have come to
affect the entire geosphere – all ecosystems, all
species.

If we blame everyone, we blame no one
we give the guilty
– free passage –
and we bear burdens we did not bring on ourselves

Some have said the Industrial Revolution. Some have said the deepening dependence upon fossil fuels coeval with the Industrial Revolution. Still others have said it's the bomb – the atomic marker registered in isotopes the world over. But the first time human activity impacted the entire planet – changing the amount of CO_2 in the atmosphere in the course of a single century – was during North American colonization, when the deaths of some 50 million indigenous inhabitants of Turtle Island was registered in a worldwide decline in CO_2 – swallowed up by the forests that filled in the farmland the indigenous worked before *they* were suddenly – swallowed up.

In the Mediterranean
fishermen sometimes
pull up skulls and bones in their nets

It's estimated there could be 50 million climate refugees by the year 2020, displaced by disasters including droughts, desertification, and floods. No matter how colonial the calculus, 50 million for 50 million is no book's balance, no ledger's line item.

we were in motion
complicating
the empty category
    – 'we' –
   moving north
sand and sea swept
in a ship al sterelees
the carapace of a beetle
blue, blue-black
midnight blue blue
of Nut and never
carried for thousands
of miles in fragile hands
to seken straunge strondes
and leave life's evidence there

the lawyer notes:
his village had been raised to the ground
he'd never been far from his home
until he wound up in London
refused asylum because they
didn't believe that he was from the tribe
he said he was from
or that his brother could be his brother

In 1816, the restored French monarchy sent a small fleet of ships, led by the frigate *Medusa*, 'to retake possession of the French establishments on the African coast.' Captained by the incompetent but loyally royalist Hugues Duroy de Chaumareys, on July 2nd the *Medusa* runs aground on the notorious Alguin Bank, off the coast of Senegal. 147 colonists and crew are set adrift on a hastily constructed raft, from which a mere 15 barely living survivors are rescued two weeks later. Madness, infighting, cannibalism, starvation, the sacrifice of the weak, and the stormy sea took the rest.

Jump ahead two centuries. On April 18ᵗʰ 2015, a massively overloaded fishing boat carrying possibly as many as 900 migrants capsizes and sinks in the Mediterranean, some 60 nautical miles off the coast of Libya, while making its way north to Italy. Only 28 survivors are pulled from the sea. Hundreds of African migrants, we learn, were locked in the submerged hold.

'Border controls are most severely deployed *by* those Western regimes that create mass displacement, and are most severely deployed *against* those whose very recourse to migration results from the ravages of capital and military occupations' (Harsha Walia, *Undoing Border Imperialism*).

'I am between hell and the deep blue sea.'

we were in motion
emptying the category
　　– 'we' –
　　moving south
serenading sinecures
in hand–made hopes
and crushing blows
an empty box
that might be filled with spice
an empty ship
that might more lightly go
if sweet and light
it could more crudely show
the underside

of the undercommons
locked deep in the hold
of the ship slipping below

In some historical situations a fire, say, is set in a building where some quarry, let's call them, has holed up, and when the quarry comes running out of the burning building they have sought, let's call it, refuge in, they are shot dead by those lying in wait who have themselves set the fire in the first place. Those who set the fire, let's call them hunters, claim the setting of the fire and the shooting of the quarry are two separate and unrelated events. They claim the quarry, whom, they accuse, were somewhere they should not have been, came running at them, and that they were therefore forced, is how they put it, to shoot them in self-defence, as they call it.

But the quarry know the direct and systemic connections between the setting of the fire and their being shot upon seeking to escape the fire – indeed, their becoming quarry, and taking refuge in the building in the first place, was the result of the hunters 'hunting'. They know this is the hunter's game, and that in this and many similar historical situations, they have so often been named quarry, and that justice is a world without hunters and without quarry, a world where fires are not lit and shots are not fired and 'the world is its own refuge.'

sea's blue
leaps out a bird
leaps out a hand

skyward to jets
to ward ships
from the shore

the lawyer
briefed and briefly
docs the
deep dislocation
in the Sahel
as rainfall patterns
floods and droughts
disrupt the
climatic fact

that the world
was born yearning
to be a home
for all

While the *Medusa* was not charged with the task of re-engaging in the slave trade, that was nevertheless the end result of the re-establishment of the French colony at Saint-Louis in Senegal, as the new governor conveniently turned the proverbial blind eye. 'By the end of June 1818, a French patrol route had been set up in an attempt to intercept and arrest slavers but, perversely, the inconvenience of eluding capture made the trade more difficult and therefore even more profitable for those who escaped the authorities.'[4]

2015 – the latch locks on the darkened hold as fighter jets scramble to fishing ports. 'Immigration restrictions and the crackdown on smugglers are part of what turned the migrant crisis into a humanitarian disaster. Instead of deterring migrants, these laws make smuggling operations more profitable, more professional and far more brutal.'[5]

Alexandre Corréard, survivor of the raft of the *Medusa* and author of *The Shipwreck of the Frigate, the Medusa*: 'Readers, who shudder at the cry of outraged humanity, recollect, at least, that it was other men, fellow countrymen and comrades, who had placed us in this abominable situation.'[6]

– declarations of rights –
whose subtle inscription
of natural life
is the ordinary figure
in this juridical order
exception made law
and life made bare

it's Zoe told me this
as we careened
through a dull day –
you can build an office
in your home
but you can't build a home
in your office

I write to the lawyer. I stare at the reproduction of the Géricault painting on the cover of Jonathan Miles's *The Wreck of the Medusa*, its greeny tones deepening in time. A mirror that turns you to stone. The energy feeding the lamp I read by. Can you really tell which bodies are white, and which are black, on the dust jacket reproduction? I scan online pictures of blue boats bobbing in the

Mediterranean, a diver dragging a blue jean-clad body up through clear water, dark hands hanging loose at its sides. I walk on the beach near my home, looking at ships and water-bound borders.

My ancestors came to the 'new world' as a new climate comes to a region that is soon warming. Coal miners, we were ourselves largely carbon, affecting other carbon, through the release of still more carbon. 'We' (things that are living) are all carbon-based beings, but 'we' (active and passive participants in waves of economic violence) don't all do unto others as 'we' would accumulate various and unequal wealths and debts to ourselves.

I say this, not to avoid race, but as a white man standing *near* the destruction, possibly for a photograph, possibly to observe (or direct). Only occasionally am I capable of being caught in the crossfire. Maybe I say the wrong thing at the wrong time, in the wrong place. Then I might be 'arrested' (and later released), or 'sued' (and the suit subsequently dropped). To get my whiteness out of the way for a moment, so the structural production/ destruction of non-white bodies may continue apace, producing wealth I (as white) may at least warm my self near.

> *I speke in prose*
> *lat him rymes make*

under immigration powers
held prior to deportation
on hunger strike until
we could prove that he was

who he said he was
from people who could speak
his language
who could confirm that he'd
been met in the village before

This was the commune
vois of every man

he lived a cold winter
sleeping in a phone box
ate food from the floor
the street market left
at the end of the day

he always asked me
about my family
even though he knew that his was gone

the law has this lingering human shape
that from its metal workings must be scraped

April 24th 2015, Senegalese writer Fatou Diome on
French television, an older white man on either
side of her, and her gallant white, male host trying
throughout to interrupt her: 'You see on the
headline the flow of African migrants arriving in
Europe but you don't speak of the Europeans going
to Africa. That's the free flow of the powerful, the
ones who have the money, and the right kind of
passports. You go to Senegal, to Mali, to any
country around the world... Anywhere I go, I meet
French people, Germans, and Dutch. I see them
everywhere around the world, because they have
the right passport. With your passport, you go

anywhere around the world, and act like you run those places, with your pretentious demeanor. Stop the hypocrisy. We will all be rich together, or perish together.' [7]

8:30am
current distance
between myself and
C. in the other room:
seven metres

8:31am
current distance
between Darfur
and London:
4850 kilometres

the earth's crust
titling under shift
of waters and ice
melt over mantle
pressing earthquake
to drought lips
this kiss for
refuge a greeting
or a goodbye

the law sits
a hooded falcon
on whose arm
privilege preys

To be granted asylum, you need a well-founded fear of persecution. In many parts of the world, for many people, this is simply called – 'everyday'. Is there an 'internal flight alternative' – that gets you outside of binaristic narratives? Largely against her will, the Man of Law's Constance would have travelled some 15,000 kilometres by sea – from Rome to Syria, to Northumbria, and back to Rome.

Syrians formed the largest group of migrants attempting to cross the Mediterranean Sea in 2014; they make their way south, into Africa, before turning north again to Libya.

A recent report claims that the US was running arms to the Syrian rebels through Benghazi. These are switches, channels made networked destruction that are traced across this Google Earth.

What if complicity is a form of relationship – of negative connection – the realisation that we are all in (or near) the same drunken boat? It's just that some of us own the boat, some of us built the boat, some of us work on the boat – some of us have boarded the boat by choice, some because we felt we had no choice, others who were given no choice at all. Still others haven't even heard about the boat, or they watch it idly, crowded and listing on TV, as waters are roughed by hovering helicopter blades. Complicity, like privilege, then, is when we find our relationship to the boat and find we were not exactly forced, that we can yet choose otherwise. Gather at the stern. Organise the disembarkation into unkempt regions of permanent asylum.

'Only from the negative impulse, from the labyrinth of the No, can the writing of the future appear' (Enrique Vila-Matas).

— asylum seeker —
oft have you to
rely on oral evidence
as to what
wilde wawes wol ye drive
or what awaits in
the place ye shal arrive

the lawyer coughs —
beneath its hood
the law startles
bells on talons jangling

accounts
can sometimes vary
and this is seen as
inconsistent
there can be different accounts
from different members of a family
and this can be seen as
inconsistent

if the information is
inconsistent
it can't be true

then there is turbulence
somewhere between
the jail and the endless sea

1819. The painter Théodore Géricault begins work
on his masterpiece, *The Raft of the Medusa*, in a
studio in suburban Paris. 'Géricault who, from the
outset, craved facts about the catastrophe and
assembled a file full of related documents' – painting

severed limbs, hands and heads in his noxious studio
– 'a tangle of limbs that recalls the human debris
strewn about the raft' – 'The painter spent days in
charnel-houses studying decay' – 'We can attribute
to these paintings and drawings of severed limbs the
role of stimuli in his living with the raft' – 'I will set
myself adrift on a difficult sea,' Géricault proclaims.[8]

The painting was 'a requiem for republican French
values.'[9] Then, as now.

1820. The painting is shown by William Bullock at
his Egyptian Hall in Piccadilly, London. Géricault
himself caving in to disease, wasting away – 'He was
so thin that he had taken on the haunting look of
a raft survivor.'[10]

October 24, 1848. In the Louvre. 'A mason's ladder
punctured *The Raft of the Medusa*, damaging some
sky and the side of the hand of the sailor waving for
rescue' – 'the controversially placed black signaller at
the apex of all their hope.'[11]

'What we see in the distance is not a rescue vessel,
it's nothing but a part of the same state machinery
that is responsible for our present plight.'[12]

– dear accomplice –
my anomic drive
is lodged in the very heart
of the *nomos*
– sing out from the
   stays and spars
   of fraught voyage –

we *shal* [not] *drenchen in the
depe*
we will be as merchants
we will prune and tame
gardens
no flowers will field us
oysters
the times will be
incipient
a chorus of groans
will mark all our small
tragedies
no one will see the eyes
we do not possess
we will not repatriate
value
value will be the heat
in our hands as we
reach out to another
and pull them onto the
shore
of this *straunge nacioun*
that is no nation at all

2015. One smuggler was a former oil rig technician.
'For the short term at least, international companies
have good reason to hunker down in Libya. The
country's crude is abundant. It is also generally light
and sweet − that is, low on density and sulfur, a
favourable formula for importers and downstream
operators − and easy to access.'[13]

The Raft of the Medusa was painted in sombre, monochromatic tones, and has grown even darker as it has aged. This the result of Géricault's experimental use of 'bituminous paint.' Bitumen: 'a naturally-occurring, non-drying, tarry substance used in paint mixtures to enrich the appearance of dark tones. Bitumen became very popular as a paint additive in the late eighteenth century and early nineteenth. However, because it does not dry it eventually causes severe darkening and cracking of the paint.'

– shapeless future –
we steal our way
far from press releases
to fish on rocks
to one side of the nothing
power does not
already oversee
practicing another mode
of gasping – intake stardust
infinitesimal drops of
water – oil
drops by turns
turned out
turning spheres colours
green turning blue
turning out

it's ok
we are always already
dead
always already
still
    rising

as Hope's more resilient daughters
Anger
    and Courage
leap from ship to shore

Libya has two seas: the Mediterranean to the north, and the Sahara to the south.

Judie, wearing a red headscarf, is from Eritrea. Aged 25, she is already a widow. She first went to Khartoum and was smuggled into Libya from there. She was caught while crossing the desert. 'Yes, it's dangerous. I know I can die. If I get a chance to live, OK, better. But if I die, that's also OK. I cannot go anywhere else to change my life.

'The four months that we stayed there – do you know what death is like? Several times they said: we're leaving. But we didn't. Twice we reached the shore but were turned back. Once we reached the boat – but then they said there's no more space.'

It looked like a fishing boat, but it was a strange time of day to go fishing. 'I will make you fishers of men,' someone somewhere once said. The ships are pointed roughly towards a certain oil rig, not far from Lampedusa. The expectation is that if the boat is not spotted earlier, the employees of the oil rig will call the Italian or Maltese Coastguard to pick it up.

'Many people would go on the boats, even if they didn't have any rescue operations.'[14]

He only turned to smuggling because he could
not find work as a lawyer

and we turn away quickly in the gallery
      damaging some sky
            and the *Grete See* seen from below
      ripples ever outward

4. Miles, Jonathan, *The Wreck of the Medusa,* New York: Atlantic Monthly Press, 2007: 221.

5. Kaplan, Sarah, 'The Real Reason for the Mediterranean Migrant Crisis,' *The Washington Post*, 21 April 2015.

6. Miles, *ibid*.: 108.

7. 'When Senegalese Author Fatou Diome Kicked European Union Butt', africaisacountry.com, 29 April 2015.

8. Miles, *ibid*.: 167-72.

9. Miles, *ibid*.: 174.

10. Miles, *ibid*.: 228.

11. Miles, *ibid*.: 243.

12. Miles, *ibid*.: 177.

13. Fortin, Jacey, 'Whatever happened to Libyan oil,' www.ibtimes.com, May 24 2013.

14. All quotations from Kingsley, Patrick, 'Libya's People Smugglers,' *The Guardian*, 24 April 2015.

The Refugee's Tale

as told to

Patience Agbabi

1

Maybe the real story begins here
in this office, before you press record
and we look in the mirror of each other's eyes, we're
first time meeting; maybe you say the word
'Refugee' in your head when you call me Farida,
Refugee, what is that burn mark on your hand?
You already have a story of the torture
I suffered in my war-torn homeland.

But these marks are from cooking bread for my family,
this is the first time I'm cooking in my life!
I never even made a cup of tea
back home. I make a very good falafel,
you must try. Are you recording? Food of the homestead:
Christians, Muslims, we bake the same flatbread.

2

Christians and Muslims break the same bread
before the change: though my parents are Egyptian,
I am born in Sudan, Sudan is in my blood.
Though I am always a Christian
even for ten years I loved Muslims
more than Christians, my Muslim neighbours
care for my parents when we jetset to Paris or Rome –
I loved Muslims as I love the Nuba;[15]

love my country, we Copts,[16] always first class,
we had good English, all of us working in the banks.
Cleaner to driver, everyone is close
to Farida, no door that is not wide open, thanks
to God, since I leave university mid-year,
and that day, I start my career.

3

The day I started my banking career,
my parents complained but they couldn't control me.
Back then was good atmosphere,
I am making good money,
my husband is running his business in patents,
we build a large family house, we have six children,
and some flats in Egypt for the pensions of our parents.
Always we are donating to the poor of our brethren.

Then government changes, doors begin to close.
At work, what took two hours now takes two weeks
and Christians are flocking overnight to the US.
Then, the rumour of a banking leak...
Watching the planes flying over my head
I refused to leave my country, my homestead.

4

I refused. I love my country, my homestead,
my mother, my father, my husband's father and mother,
the motherland; I would rather be buried dead
than leave, I was the last one to leave: my brother-
in-law, he's unwell, he needed support to heal
his divided mind, we nurture him like a plant
and polish each leaf, each flower to help seal
him together − like the two faiths that can't

be divided by politicians completely corrupted,
splitting the country like an open wound: they insert
a lie and there's Christians abducted.
I refused to cover my hair but my heart
was divided by language, river, boundary, country,
the day I retreated my status to refugee.

5

Why should I be treated as stranger, as refugee
in the country I was born, barricaded in
my bank, while demonstrators outside shout blasphemy,
hundreds, thousands fed with propaganda poison.
We're told, Remain calm, stay here, you have food
but my phone buzzed like a dying insect −
my husband, my children, my parents pleading with God.
I remembered the side-door, the back exit

where the generator hummed in the dark
and I find myself descending the iron stairs,
the noise of the crowd out front like a bull shark
and somehow my legs find the car, my hands on the gears
and my friend is closing the door imagining the crowbar
fists of the crowd pounding on my car.

6

The fist-headed crowd are pounding on my car.
My car is not moving. Each fist has a face
that looks like my own. How can we be at war
when the Nile flows through our twin faiths?
If my car is my coffin,
their fists are the clods of earth, the rich yellow soil
of my country. I start the engine,
praying, Dear God, let it… let it not stall…

But my car is the black and the steel
of a bulletproof jacket, today it will save
my life, with my hands on the steering wheel
and my life in the hand of God, it begins to move
and the waving fists part like the Red Sea.
I still think it's miracle I find myself free.

7

It's miracle I'm still having job but my mind is not free:
each day government is ringing for bank information
that I am not having. They don't believe me.
More doors are closed in my face with no explanation.
Maybe somewhere there's a typed memo,
on a blank piece of paper someone has printed my name,
someone is watching my house, how, I don't know,
anger is a gloved hand and a flickering flame.

That night, the family is sleeping on the second floor
except my oldest son and daughter coming back
from coptic club: they open the side-door
and all they are smelling is smoke… Someone broke
into our life, their hand through our window bars
that night, to smother the moon and stars.

8

The night smoke choked the moon and the stars
I tried to call the fire... I tried to call them
hundreds of times. If it wasn't for our neighbours
hearing us shouting... my neighbours came
and there was water... I shouted like crazy,
Please, please help us at this address,
and nobody came. Like they arranged it, maybe,
the fire brigade not to come, and we all perish.

My husband insisted to break the room and go inside
and the flames... I was so worried about him...
but my neighbours... all my family survived.
We prayed there together, Christian and Muslim,
in the heat of the fire, we knelt on the earth, and wept.
I thought I forget but their love I'll never forget.

9

I thought I forget in this life but I never forget
the three hours it took for the fire engine to arrive
felt like three days. There is no regret,
we were lucky to be alive.
But how can you sleep, then, knowing the country you love
wants you to die, how can you close your eyes shut
when they've been pitted like an olive?
I'm praying to God every night but

then after that, they started with my husband.
He was away with his business abroad,
they arrested him at Customs
coming back to our country, his papers ignored.
He sense something bad would... had a premonition...
the day they imprison my husband, he had not eaten.

10

They put my husband in prison, he is not eating
the right foods, they knew he was diabetic
but they're starving him of insulin,
wouldn't let me give his medicine, I was frantic.
I didn't know where he was based,
didn't know what they can do to him to get me
and finally I decided there was no way... I could not... resist.
That's when I decided to leave my beloved country.

They said, you should be grateful we left you in peace,
this is a Muslim country but we let you pray
in your churches. Cooperate for your husband's release.
I know nothing of that bank information to this day.
Always I am wearing my cross and refused to sweat
in the heavy black and steel of my bulletproof jacket.

11

The heavy black and steel of a bulletproof jacket
is the depression I wear on the worse days
when freedom here weighs heavier than the death threat
back home and my family fall on their knees.
But back home I refused, why should Farida wear widow's
black when there is still hope for my husband
to bend the bars on his prison windows.
Always, there's light on the horizon.

I knew a Muslim high official, a friend
of my husband. Farida, trust me, I have a plan.
So I'm buying us tickets to London, even then
thinking we can come back when things cool down.
The day of his release, I'm barely breathing:
meeting him at the airport, the sky is bleeding.

12

When I met him at the airport... he was bleeding...
his chest was full of blood... and he had
ulcerative colitis, he is needing
urgent medical... very sick... he bled
onto the flight... and is sleeping very peaceful
and the whole of my family is here and safe.
As soon as we land we take him to hospital
and... they save his life.

An international visa is an open door
but the next day we go to Croydon to claim asylum
and though the lady is very kind it pains me more
than everything to cut myself from my home,
my country, with each section of my claim.
My story... depressed photo in a frame.

13

The story depends where you put the frame:
with my oldest son, my oldest daughter
each in a separate room, but exactly the same
questions, each the author
of a story they will match to see if the grief
fits together the jigsaw of what it is
to love your country and be forced to leave
your whole life behind in broken images.

For me it was lucky, maybe God knows how much I suffered;
maybe it was easy to check my job, my contacts;
maybe the fictions in the newspapers
were detained by the facts.
Now I'm underclass, my head covered with shame.
~~How am I begging when I can't remember my name?~~

14

How can I begin to remember my name
when I can't leave the house… when the ache of leaving
my mother… she died… the blame
is too much… my whole body drowned with grieving
in this room, with the ribbed roof, where I sit with my sins
heavy as Jonah… this silent attic
where memories play back like the cries of muezzins
mixed with the cries from the priests when she first fell sick?

But good people come, who open me to feel
again for others; and as I translate the words
of a refugee life to a form, I begin to heal.
Their voice is my own voice striking a chord.
May our truth conquer fear:
maybe the real story begins here.

15

Maybe the real story begins here:
when Christians and Muslims broke the same flatbread;
the day I started my banking career
and refused to leave my country, my homestead;
maybe the day I retreated my status to refugee;
or the fist-headed crowd pounding on my car
and the miracle when I find myself free;
the night the smoke choked the moon and stars.

I thought I forget but some things you never forget:
the day they imprison my husband, he is not eating;
the heavy black and steel of my bulletproof jacket
when I met him at the airport, broken, bleeding.
The story ends where you put the frame:
but however it begins, remember my name.

---

15. Inhabitants of the Nuba Mountains of South Kordofan State, in Sudan.
16. Christian denomination mainly found in Egypt but also in Sudan and Libya.

Afterword

Walking with Refugee Tales

Setting

As THE SUBTITLE OF the original project had it, *Refugee Tales* was 'A Walk in Solidarity with Refugees, Asylum Seekers and Detainees (from Dover to Crawley via Canterbury)'. The route was the North Downs Way, which largely coincides with the Pilgrims' Way, being the ancient track along which people once travelled from Hampshire (and points in between) to Canterbury. Organised by Gatwick Detainees Welfare Group (in collaboration with Kent Refugee Help), the walk took nine days, punctuated, at every stop, by the public telling of two tales: one, the tale of an asylum seeker, former immigration detainee or refugee; the other of a person – for instance a lawyer or interpreter – who works with people seeking asylum in the UK. Each tale was a collaboration between an established writer and the person whose tale was being told and the overarching purpose of the project was to call for an immediate end to indefinite immigration detention in the UK. Drawing, structurally, on *The Canterbury Tales*, the project thus had three fundamental elements: a culturally charged sense of space, the visible fact of human movement, and an exchange of information through the act of telling stories. It is interesting also to note the dates of the project: 13th–21st June, 2015.

Dates matter. When *Refugee Tales* took place it was ahead

of the historical curve – only just, as it turned out, but ahead nonetheless. For those who witnessed it, the sight of (at any one point) between 80 and 150 people, a good number of whom were asylum seekers and ex-detainees, crossing the landscapes of southern England, was a powerful spectacle. The point of the spectacle – it came to be understood as a spectacle of welcome – was that people who are hidden by and from the culture, rendered invisible by the procedures of the state, were here taking and asserting their places in the landscape. The project was blessed by the weather – it only rained once – and so there were days when it was possible to see the whole party strung out across the countryside, walkers in solidarity stretched a mile or more into the distance. It is this aspect of the project, its sheer conspicuousness, that has most been altered by subsequent events, though it is important to register a shifting chronology.

At the moment of the project, reporting on the so-called 'migrant crisis' was concentrated on Calais. The repeated images, on which organisers were invited to comment, were of people running alongside vehicles or climbing into lorries, and the tone of the reporting was one of hostility. That was June 2015. By mid-August the images had decisively altered. The sight of tens of thousands of refugees – or people seeking asylum – walking through Hungary towards Germany and other parts of Northern Europe, became the trigger for a notably different tone and, temporarily at least, the makings of a different discourse. As the project relates to this historical event, the consequence is that it can't ever look the same. When *Refugee Tales* walks again, as it will in July 2016, and in so far as it achieves a visual impact, it will be walking after the historical fact.

In crucial respects, however, the geopolitical shift effected by the so-called 'migrant crisis' makes the *Refugee Tales* project, which is to say the space it opened up, all the more consequential. We mean space in the larger, metaphorical sense, in the sense of a cultural and political environment.

There is, however, a more literal sense of space that the project addresses, and to understand that sense we need to know a little about the processes of immigration detention, and about detention and post-detention existence.

Detention

In theory, typically at least, a person is held in immigration detention at the point at which they are imminently to be removed from the UK. This arrangement, which is to say the detention, is temporary, but it is also indefinite. The consequence is that a person who is not at that point charged with any crime can be detained for months or years, pending their removal. At the recently closed Dover Immigration Removal Centre, for example, the longest period of detention was over four years. Pending is the word. We are deep, here, within the lexicon of suspension. Following that period of indefinite detention, some people, less than half as it turns out, will actually be removed. The others, for whatever reason, often to do with the impossibility of securing travel documents, will be 'released' back into the community. Once released some will be accommodated in Section 4 bail accommodation, which the conditions of their bail will specify they have to return to every night (a requirement sometimes reinforced by an electronic tag). Since people who have been detained, former detainees, can't work, they receive a form of relief paid not in cash but in the form of vouchers called an Azure card; a form of top-up card that can only be used in certain shops or supermarkets and which (as The British Red Cross reported in 2014) carries certain restrictions including, crucially, the fact that it can't be spent on public transport.

There are other functions of the Azure card, more symbolic, to do with the relation it establishes between the ex-detainee and the currency. A person using an Azure card in a supermarket is quickly picked out as somebody outside the cultural norm; like wearing a badge, a visible marker of difference. The restriction on public transport, however, is among the most material effects, one consequence being that when they have to report at a Home Office Reporting Centre (on a weekly, fortnightly or monthly basis, depending on the conditions of their release from detention) many former detainees will have to walk long distances just to make the report. The more general effect, however, is to fix a person in a given location, often for months and years on end (over a decade is not at all uncommon). Except that with that stasis – again, part of the lexicon of detention – comes the risk that at any point they might be 'dispersed' (relocated to another part of the country), or re-detained (which is common). The result of all of the above is that ex-detainees (who are frequently so-called failed asylum seekers, but who might sometimes, perhaps years later, secure refugee status) have a deeply compromised relation to public space.

We will come back to this compromised relation to space, and to the ways, in its occupation of the landscape, *Refugee Tales* sought to address the question. We will come back also to the word 'structurally' because one thing, above all maybe, that reading the whole series of tales confirms is that in the asylum system there are no accidents. That for all the seeming confusion of the processes, and the ad hoc nature of the determinations, the effect on the individual, of deep and protracted demoralisation (to put it politely), is systematic. For the moment, though, having mentioned space, it is necessary to register the detainee's relation to time.

To be clear: an Immigration Removal Centre is a place where people who have come to the UK, many seeking refuge, and whose rights of appeal have apparently been exhausted, pending removal are indefinitely detained. Some (but by no means all) of the people detained will have committed a crime, for which they will already have served the required prison sentence. Frequently such crimes will be asylum-related, for instance attempting to leave the country by false papers; a somewhat contradictory misdemeanour, on the face of it, since the country has made it plain it doesn't want such people to stay. Other detainees will have reached a legal limit, such as those who first arrived in the UK as unaccompanied minors, typically from countries affected by war such as Afghanistan or Iraq, and whose entitlement to stay expires when they turn 18. Having lived here since he was 15 (having left Afghanistan when his father was executed by the Taliban), Gulab was detained without warning, waking one night to find his room in South London occupied by more than 20 border police. As Theresa Hayter puts it, in *Open Borders*, 'People may be picked up in the street, on the underground or at work, or their houses may be raided in the early hours.' Following which, pending deportation, they are indefinitely detained. Durations vary. Turnaround times can be as little as two to three days. In the past decade periods of detention (often followed by further periods of re-detention) have quite commonly been between six months and two years. As was widely reported at the time, at the end of 2012, Nick Hardwick, the Chief Inspector of Prisons, discovered a Somali man in Lincoln Prison who had been held in immigration detention for nine years.

Under British criminal law, it is not permissible to detain a person indefinitely. In normal circumstances the maximum period a person can be detained without charge is 24 hours, rising to 96 hours (four days), 'if a serious crime is suspected.' The only exception to these limits relates to persons suspected of terrorism, who, under special powers granted by the 2006 Terrorism Act could be detained for up to 28 days. This length of time was fiercely contested at the point of its introduction and the temporary powers granting it were allowed to lapse in 2011, the period of detention reverting to its pre-2006 limit of 14 days. The significance of these periods lies in the sense of a limit, a limit that relates to the question of sovereignty and that ties the question of sovereignty to the issue of time. The question cuts both ways. Sovereign law establishes its ethical character by the degree to which it encroaches on, and also protects, the sovereign actions of the individual citizen. Currently one key measure of that relationship in the UK is the period of 14 days, being the point beyond which the interests of the individual cannot be overridden by the interests of the state. Unless, that is, the individual is held in immigration detention. This begs the question: how is the institution of the removal centre legal? Or rather, since, in conventional terms, it plainly offends legal principles, what relation does such a site have to the law? The answer is that it seems to stand just outside: subject to the law's authority but not governed by its defining protections; a setting where different rules of sovereignty and temporality apply.[17]

Walking

It is against this background that the *Refugee Tales* project occupied the landscape the way it did. It mattered a lot that the walk followed ancient pathways, that it cut across tracts of southern England intimately connected to a national view. It is in these spaces as much as any – Kent, Surrey, Sussex – and in the idiom of these spaces, that the language of national identity forms and perpetuates, functioning as it does to hold the migrant out of view. Serviceable as that language of national identity might once have been as a way of organising a relation to space, what the events of last summer show – though we surely knew it already – is that such a way of orienting ourselves to space badly needs to be re-made. *Refugee Tales* was one form of that re-making: the crossing of a deeply national space by people whom the nation has organised itself in order precisely that they be kept from view.

There are many implications of this changed relation to space, not the least being the way we think about cultural expression. Take Chaucer, for instance, the father of English poetry, but in whom the writers involved in the project found a deeply complicated geography. What a number of writers became pre-occupied with was 'The Man of Law's Tale', the events of which see an Italian Princess taken to Syria, from which regime she is banished by being set adrift on the Mediterranean, eventually to arrive in the North of England – 'Northumbria' – where subsequently she is falsely accused of a crime. This is to simplify both the original tale and the writers' interest in it, but it is also to indicate a political geography in Chaucer that intervenes deeply on any assumption of a national frame. Or consider the great opening sentence of 'The General Prologue' – 'Whan that Aprill with his shoures soote' – with its seemingly deeply rooted sense of climate and environment, but in which, even before such rootedness has bedded down, one is introduced to the pleasure and necessity of movement:

> And palmeres for to seken straunge strondes,
> To ferne halwes, kowthe in sondry londes.'
> ('And palmers to visit foreign shores
> To distant shrines, well known in different lands')

Deep within the *Refugee Tales* project is a proposal that the language of national space be re-read, that we read back through to find the expression that gestures outwards.

There is, however, also, a simpler thing to say about the way *Refugee Tales* occupied its space from the 13th-21st June, which is that – for the duration at least – people involved were more at ease. Thus, for all that the tales themselves focused attention on traumatic and unjust events, the walk itself was charged with something like relief. For those among the party who had been detained, this sense of relief came – as was variously said – from the fact of being out and about, a way of being in space that for some hadn't been available in several years. For others in the *Refugee Tales* group, let's call them people whose rights of residence were not under scrutiny, the relief came of occupying a space in a way that was not governed by the prevailing discourse. For the duration of the walk there was a relation to space that seemed, as the project walked, to be ethically sustainable.

Tales

For the person who visits a detention centre, it is a striking element of the process that one is not allowed to carry a pen and paper into the building. In one respect this is a catch-all policy; a person's pockets have to be emptied. In another respect, this holding of the detainee and the ex-detainee outside the language is replicated across the asylum system. One sees an echo in the voucher system, the individual held symbolically outside the currency. More explicitly, it is a surprise to discover that the immigration bail hearing, one of the few mechanisms by which an individual might be released from detention, is not a hearing of record. The judge asks a series of questions, but nobody is writing the questions, or the answers, down. Nobody, that is, except in recent times, the excellent Bail Observation Project, realising as they did the necessity for documentation. More than this, the detainee himself or herself is typically not present in the hearing, but is relayed, by a video-link, from the detention centre itself. The effect of this video relay is, inevitably, significantly to diminish the presence of the individual, to make their appeal, as a person, easier to ignore. More surprisingly still, given what is at stake in the occasion, the asylum appeal is not a hearing of record either. There will be a written determination, composed by the judges, but the exchanges themselves, the questions put by the Home Office for instance – that's all off record.

It is this fact, the holding of people outside the skin of the language, that principally motivated *Refugee Tales*, inspired, as the project was, by Gatwick Detainee Welfare Group's 20 years' experience of visiting and talking with people who have been detained. The content of the tales is paramount of course, as you have seen, but the process of composition was also important. To outline that process, with the exception of 'The Lorry Driver's Tale' (where the interviews had already taken place), each writer talked at length with the person or people whose tale it was, either in person or where necessary – as in the case of 'The Deportee's Tale' – by phone. In each case, the writer was invited to take the necessary formal decisions towards a 20 minute performance. Equally, the tale had to be grounded in the reality of the experience that the person's original telling presented.

To understand what's at stake in such a telling we need some background thoughts. The question, obviously, is why should people not simply have told their own tales; the question being most pressing in the case of the asylum seekers, refugees and former detainees. There are two principal answers to this question. The first is that, in a number of cases, the person concerned remained so traumatised by the events that had caused them to make their journey, and also, subsequently, by the treatment they had experienced in the UK, that it would have been inappropriate (simply not possible in practice) for them to speak in front of an audience of between 100 and 200 people. The second reason was that, given the constant risk of re-detention, those who had been detained did not want their names attached to their tales. To be clear, they very much wanted their tales to be told, but not in a way that might identify them. Anonymity was at a premium because, in the UK, people in the asylum system fear reprisal.

There is much that might be said about this narrative dynamic. Two things in particular, however, should be remarked on, by way of context. One is the fact that to tell another person's tale one has to listen at length and very closely; at such length, in fact, that the experience being relayed grafts onto and alters the listener's language. This is what the writers reported; that having collaborated in the way they did their relation to the language was significantly changed. More importantly, there is a thing that the people whose tales were being told, repeatedly said. What variously they said about the process was that it was a relief that the tale was being told, though for the reasons given above they could not, in the immediacy of the moment, be the person who told it. More subtly, what people said was that they were relieved the account was being passed on. What that passing on of a story means, in this context, is a matter for some consideration. What perhaps it means is that a story that belongs to one person now belongs, also, to other people; that other people acknowledge the experience that constitutes the story, but also that in making that acknowledgment they register responsibility. These are tales, in other words, that call for and generate a collective; tales that need to be told and re-told so that the situation they emerge from might be collectively addressed.

What this telling and re-telling of other people's tales points to is the metaphorical sense of space mentioned at the outset, the cultural space that *Refugee Tales* hoped to help open up. Here again, there are various things to say. The first is that the set piece telling of tales was hardly the only way in which stories were communicated. One of the most powerful forms of exchange took place at the Friends' Meeting House in Rochester, when the walkers participated in a roundtable discussion addressing the question: what does it mean to be welcomed? It was an occasion when people who had been detained articulated clearly and at length what detention was. Similarly, the final performance of the project, at the Hawth Theatre in Crawley, featured a dramatic representation of 'The Ex-Detainee's Tale'; a piece in which people previously detained took the metamorphosis of Kafka's Gregor Samsa as a starting point for articulating the effect of detention on an individual life. A further thing to say is that this whole dynamic of storytelling is not sufficient; that plainly it must be the objective of a project such as *Refugee Tales* to question any aspect of mediation, including its own; that it must seek to create the circumstance in which anonymity is not a shaping conceit. But the last thing to say is that for all the shifts in the discourse around migration that have followed the current crisis, the question of indefinite detention, a cornerstone of UK immigration policy, has remained almost entirely absent from the debate. The principal intention of *Refugee Tales* was to help communicate the scandalous reality of detention and post-detention existence to a wider audience and in the process to demand that such indefinite detention ends. Further demands follow: the entitlement to work and the entitlement to be educated; the entitlement, in other words, for a life not to be held brutally in suspense. Various forms of pressure will be required to achieve these objectives, but key to those pressures, certainly, will be the circulation of stories. Whatever else, the language needs to change.

David Herd, December 2015

---

17. This account of conditions in detention and post-detention is accurate at the time of writing. The forthcoming immigration bill, due to become law in 2016, proposes to make such conditions a great deal worse.

About the Contributors

Patience Agbabi has performed her poetry all over the world. She is celebrated for her monologues, giving voice to those who might be otherwise unheard. She has published four collections of poetry. In 2013, 'The Doll's House', based on Harewood House, was shortlisted for the Forward Prize for Best Single Poem. She has lectured in several UK universities and has been a Fellow in Creative Writing at Oxford Brookes University since 2008. She was made Canterbury Laureate and received an Arts Council England 'Grants for the Arts' award to write her fourth collection, a Canterbury Tales for the 21st century. *Telling Tales* (Canongate, 2014) was shortlisted for the Ted Hughes Award for New Work in Poetry 2014 and 2015 Wales Book of the Year.

Jade Amoli-Jackson lives in Clapham Junction. Following her degree, she worked as a sports reporter on television and radio, and on national and local papers. Her sister, father and other family members were killed by government soldiers and, with her own life in danger, she arrived in the UK as a refugee in July 2001. She is a member of the Medical Foundation's Write To Life group and published her first collection of poetry, *Moving A Country*, in 2013, edited by Tom Green and Lucy Popescu and supported by Platforma. Jade has also performed work at the Battersea Arts Centre and Tate galleries. She has been a volunteer at the Refugee Council since 2005.

Chris Cleave is a novelist and former columnist for *The Guardian*. His debut novel *Incendiary* (Chatto & Windus, 2005) won a 2006 Somerset Maugham Award, was shortlisted for the 2006 Commonwealth Writers Prize, won the United States Book-of-the-Month Club's First Fiction award 2005, and won the Prix Spécial du Jury at the French Prix des Lecteurs 2007. Inspired by his childhood in West Africa and by an accidental visit to a British concentration camp, Chris Cleave's second novel is entitled *The Other Hand* (Sceptre, 2008) in the UK, Australia, New Zealand and South Africa. It is entitled *Little Bee* in the US and Canada. His new novel, *Everyone Brave is Forgive* was published by Simon & Schuster earlier this year. He has been variously a barman, a long-distance sailor, a teacher of marine navigation, an internet pioneer and a journalist.

Stephen Collis is a poet, editor and professor. His many books of poetry include *The Commons* (Talon, 2008; second edition 2014), *On the Material* (Talon, 2010 – awarded the BC Book Prize for Poetry), *To the Barricades* (Talon, 2013) and, with Jordan Scott, *DECOMP* (Coach House, 2013). He has also written two books of literary criticism, a book of essays on the Occupy Movement, *Dispatches from the Occupation* (Talon, 2012), and a novel, *The Red Album* (BookThug, 2013). In 2014, while involved in anti-pipeline activism, he was sued for $5.6 million by US energy giant Kinder Morgan, whose lawyers read his writing in court as 'evidence'. His forthcoming book is *Once in Blockadia* (Talon, 2016). He lives near Vancouver, on unceded Coast Salish Territory, and teaches at Simon Fraser University.

Born in Nigeria, **Inua Ellams** is a poet, playwright, performer, graphic artist and designer. He is a Complete Works poet alumni and a graphic designer at White Space Creative Agency. He facilitates workshops in creative writing and has been recognised with a number of awards, most recently, the Live Canon International Poetry Prize, an Arts Council England Award, and a Wellcome Trust Award. He has been shortlisted for the Brunel Prize for African Poetry, longlisted for the Alfred Fagan Award, and won a 2009 Edinburgh Fringe First Award. He has been commissioned by Tate Modern, Louis Vuitton, Chris Ofili, the National Theatre, BBC Radio and Television, Battersea Arts Centre and Soho Theatre. His first two books of poetry, *Thirteen Fairy Negro Tales* (2005) and *Candy Coated Unicorn and Converse All Stars* (2011), are available from Flipped Eye, and several plays including *Black T-shirt Collection* and *Knight Watch* are available from Oberon (both 2012). In 2005, he founded the Midnight Run, a cross art form nocturnal urban movement to reconnect inner city lives with inner city spaces.

Abdulrazak Gurnah was born in 1948 in Zanzibar and teaches at the University of Kent. He is the author of seven novels, including *Paradise* (Hamish Hamilton, 1994), which was shortlisted for both the Booker and the Whitbread Prizes, *By the Sea* (Bloomsbury, 2001), longlisted for the Booker Prize and awarded the RFI Temoin du monde prize), and *Desertion* (Bloomsbury, 2005), shortlisted for the Commonwealth Prize.

David Herd is a poet, critic, and teacher. His collections of poetry include *All Just* (Carcanet, 2012), *Outwith* (BookThug, 2012), and *Through* (Carcanet, 2016), and his recent writings on the politics of human movement have appeared in *The Los Angeles Review of Books*, *Parallax* and *Almost Island*. He is Professor of Modern Literature at the University of Kent, has worked with Kent Refugee Help since 2009, and is a co-ordinator of *Refugee Tales*.

Marina Lewycka was born of Ukrainian parents in a refugee camp in Kiel, Germany, after World War II, and now lives in Sheffield, Yorkshire. Her first novel, *A Short History of Tractors in Ukrainian* (Viking, 2005) was published when she was 58 years old, and went on to sell a million copies in 35 languages. It was shortlisted for the 2005 Orange Prize for Fiction, longlisted for the Man Booker prize, won the 2005 Saga Award for Wit and the 2005 Bollinger Everyman Wodehouse Prize for Comic Fiction. Her second novel, *Two Caravans* (Viking, 2007) (published in the US as *Strawberry Fields*), was shortlisted for the George Orwell prize for political writing. *We Are All Made of Glue*, her third novel, was published in 2009; *Various Pets Alive and Dead* in 2012, and her new novel *The Lubetkin Legacy* is due out in May 2016 (all from Penguin).

Avaes Mohammad works across poetry, theatre and performance. With a background in the chemical sciences, his influences stretch from the Sufi-Saints of South Asia to the Dub-Poets of Jamaica. His poem 'Bhopal', as commissioned by BBC Radio 4, won an Amnesty International Media Award. He has been commissioned by BBC Radio and several theatre companies across the country, to write such plays as *Bhopal* (2003), *In God We Trust* (2005), *The Student* (2007), *Shadow Companion* (2008), *Crystal Kisses* (2010/2011), *Fields of Grey* (2012) and *Of Another World* (2014). He was recently commissioned to write a double-bill for the Park Theatre, London. In 2012, he co-founded The Lahore Agitprop Theatre Company in Pakistan. Constantly excited by how his work as an artist can support society, he is currently Associate Artist with Red Ladder Theatre Company, Fellow of the Muslim Institute and Trustee of the Bhopal Medical Appeal.

After 40 years of teaching, **Hubert Moore** was for nine years a writing mentor at the Medical Foundation for the Care of Victims of Torture, now Freedom from Torture. At the same time he was a regular visitor of detainees at Dover Detention Centre. His eighth collection of poems, *The Bright Gaze of the Disoriented,* was recently published by Shoestring Press in 2014. His poem 'Hosing Down' was Highly Commended in last year's Forward Prize list.

Anna Pincus, a founder and co-ordinator of *Refugee Tales*, has worked for Gatwick Detainees Welfare Group for ten years, supporting people held in immigration detention and the volunteers who visit them, managing outreach work and campaigning to end indefinite detention.

Ali Smith was born in Inverness in 1962 and lives in Cambridge. She is the author of *Public Library and Other Stories* (Hamish Hamilton, 2015), *How to be Both* (Hamish Hamilton, 2014), *Artful, There But For The* (Hamish Hamilton, 2011), *Free Love* (Virago, 1995), *Like*, (Virago, 1997), *Hotel World* (Hamish Hamilton, 2001), *Other Stories and Other Stories* (Granta, 1999), *The Whole Story and Other Stories* (Hamish Hamilton, 2003), *The Accidental* (Hamish Hamilton, 2005), *Girl Meets Boy* (Canongate, 2007), and *The First Person and Other Stories* (Hamish Hamilton, 2008). *Hotel World* was shortlisted for the Booker Prize and the Orange Prize, and *The Accidental* was shortlisted for the Man Booker Prize and the Orange Prize. *How to be Both* won the Baileys Women's Prize for Fiction, the Costa Novel of the Year, and the Goldsmiths Prize, and was shortlisted for the Man Booker Prize and the Folio Prize.

Dragan Todorovic is the author of ten books of fiction, non-fiction, and poetry, and has contributed to several collections. His novel *Diary of Interrupted Days* (Random House, 2009) was shortlisted for the Commonwealth Writers' Prize, Amazon First Novel Award and other awards. His memoir *The Book of Revenge* (Vintage, 2007) won the Nereus Writers' Trust Non-Fiction Prize and was shortlisted for British Columbia's National Award for Canadian Non-Fiction. His interactive poetry project, *Five Walks on Isabella Street*, won the 1998 Astound International Competition. Several of his works have been anthologised. Dragan has written and directed numerous radio plays, TV documentaries and hosted over 150 live TV interviews (on Culture Channel and 3K, Serbia). His aural essay, 'In My Language I am Smart', was performed on CBC Radio One and published on a CD in 2012. Dragan teaches Creative Writing at the University of Kent in Canterbury.

A poet and critic, **Carol Watts** is Professor of Literature and Poetics at Birkbeck, University of London. Her poetry includes the collections *Many Weathers Wildly Comes* (Spiralbound/ Susakpress 2015), *Sundog* (Veer Books, 2013), *Occasionals* (Reality Street Editions, 2011), and *Wrack* (Reality Street Editions, 2007), and a number of artist's books. Her chapbooks include the series *When Blue Light Falls* (Oystercatcher, 2008, 2010, 2012), *This Is Red* (Torque Press, 2009) and the sonnet sequences *Mother Blake* (2012) and *Brass, Running* (2006), both with Equipage. She often works collaboratively, most recently with George Szirtes on an exchange called *56*, which will be published by Arc in 2016. She would like to thank the anonymous translator whose careful, generous conversation shaped 'The Interpreter's Tale'.

Michael Zand is a writer, editor and researcher. He was born in Iran, but has spent most of his life in London, where he is now Visiting Lecturer in Creative Writing at the University of Roehampton. His research interests lie in alternative translations of Middle Eastern poetry, the use of psycho-geography in contemporary literature, and modern readings of the medieval notion of the 'Ashik', or wandering poet. His collections include *Kval* (Arthur Shilling, 2009) and *Lion: The Iran Poems* (Shearsman, 2010). He was included in the *Best Poetry of 2011* anthology (Salt, 2011) and won the Roehampton Poetry Performance Prize in 2008. His latest collection, *The Wire and Other Poems*, was published by Shearsman Books in 2012. He is currently working on a contemporary translation of *The Rubaiyat of Omar Khayyam* entitled 'Ruby'. In February 2013, his sequence of poems entitled 'Pang' was included in an exhibition on *Poets of the Thames* at the Museum of English Rural Life in Reading, Berkshire.

Special Thanks

The editors would like to thank everyone the Gatwick Detainees Welfare Group has worked with in detention, whose stories inspired *Refugee Tales*. The project was the work of many hands. Thanks to the writers and to those who shared their tales. Thanks to the chairs of the *Refugee Tales* committees, Mary Barrett and Christina Fitzsimons, thanks to the *Refugee Tales* committee members and thank you to our Patron, Ali Smith. Thanks to GDWG volunteers, GDWG staff and trustees. Thank you to Sarah Pailthorpe and the catering team. Thanks to the support crew, walk leaders, drivers, chaperones, logo and website designers, web-master, photographers and film-makers. Thanks for the welcome at the venues, village halls and church halls that hosted us. Thank you to the compères, guest speakers and round-table participants. Thank you to Sam Bailey and the musicians. Thanks to Bridges Arts Group and the London Nautical School, to the storyteller, Northbourne CEP School and to Sholden CEP School. Thanks to Kent Refugee Help, Kent Refugee Action Network, the University of Kent, Refugee Week, Platforma Arts, Music in Detention, Samphire, the *Refugee Tales* patrons, Arts Council England, Awards for All, and the Dover Big Local. Thanks to Ra Page and Comma Press for their commitment to the project, and thank you to everybody who walked.